HOLY POISON

Book Two

THE FLAWED MISTRESS

Rachel's Journal

by

Margaret Brazear

http://www.historical-romance.com

D0573417

The Final Confession of Lord Richard Summerville is not available to the general public. Find out how you can have access **to this hidden document**

CHAPTER ONE

Rachel's Journal

Were anyone to ask me about my childhood, I would have to reply that I did not have one, at least not one that I can remember. I was born Lady Rachel Stewart, the child of an impoverished earl, a man who had gambled and drunk away his entire fortune, and that of his three wives, the last of which was my mother. When I came along there was little left and by the time I was ten, there was nothing.

I recall lying in bed at night and hearing the quarrel about money, Father telling Mother that he had found a way to pay off all his debts and have a lot left over, her protesting, begging him not to do it. I had no notion of what this was all about, and I did not want to know, so I buried my head beneath the covers and stopped up my ears before the blows started falling, before my father got his whip with which to persuade her that he was right.

All I remember of my father is that I feared him. He had never hurt me as such; he never paid me that much attention, but he was violent toward my mother on a daily basis. Whatever went wrong, it was her fault and she took the punishment for it. I did not know then, of course, that the beatings she took were often caused by her defence of me; to keep him away from me she had put herself in the way.

Children never know these things. They just take it for granted that this is how things are and I probably assumed that this was the way things were in every family.

All I knew was that we were all safer if I kept out of his way. If I made him angry, my mother would be hurt. He had no interest in me, or so I believed, and that suited me well.

I was completely innocent then, knowing nothing of the world or even how babies were born. I was just a child and things would not have been spoken about in front of me, not even if Mother had anyone to talk to.

She only had me and the servants, but nothing could be confided to them. They knew precisely what went on, as servants always do, but they feared my father as much as my mother and I did.

My earliest memory is that of my tenth birthday, of watching my father fill himself full of strong wine and listening to my mother's weeping from her bedchamber. I had no idea why she was crying more than usual, but a huge carriage arrived early in the morning and made her wails even worse. It was as if the very sight of that carriage hurt her somehow.

The gentleman who stepped out of the carriage was old, not only by my own standards but elderly by the standards of the time. He was, in fact, my father's age with similar grey hair and lined face, although without the bloated face and body that my father had acquired through drink.

His clothing declared him to be wealthy. He wore a doublet of red satin, with rich embroidery and encrusted jewels. His hose was silk and on his gnarled fingers he wore many rings, too many for simple decoration and good taste. He could have done a lot of damage with those rings, should anyone challenge him.

I was watching from the gallery when he entered, when he strode passed the servant who stepped forward to show him in to see my father, and into the great hall itself. If I had known then that this man was to be the cause of all the misery to come in my life, I would have run away and hid somewhere, never come out of my hiding place.

But I did not know, nor could I guess at the motive for his visit. I was too young then to even imagine what he might want, too young to know that there was anything more evil than my father and his whip.

"Well," the stranger demanded. "I have the money. Have you decided yet? I cannot wait forever."

He threw a velvet purse down on the table and my father took it and opened it up to look inside, while his eyes grew wide and greedy.

"It is all there," the stranger said. "One thousand gold pieces as we agreed, as well as all your debts paid." He watched my father for a few seconds, then added with a smirk of satisfaction: "Not bad for a loan of one day. She had better be worth it."

My father nodded, then got up and came to the bottom of the stairs, calling my name.

"Rachel," he called. "I have a special birthday present for you. Come down here."

I moved slowly down the stairs, not wanting to trip and disgrace myself, but also because I did not feel very safe in the company of this man. I had never felt safe in the company of my father, but that was because he got drunk and became violent. There was something else about this man that made me afraid, although I could not have said what. I was too young then to know; I would know now.

"This is Mr Carter, my dear," my father went on. "He is a friend and he wants to take you out for the day to celebrate your birthday. Is that not good of him?"

I remember shaking my head in mute refusal. I did not want to go with him and even my ten year old mind could not fathom why this stranger might want to take me out. Perhaps he had no children of his own, I tried to tell myself, but even as I thought it, something told me that was not the reason.

I heard my mother crying from the top of the stairs.

"No! You cannot take her!"

My father climbed the stairs then, faster than I thought possible in an old man so unfit. I turned to look, turned in time to see him strike my mother across the face, hard, tearing her cheek with his ring. It was not the first time I had witnessed that particular scene and I did not know then that it would be the last, but on this occasion that was all I saw, because Mr Carter had grabbed my arm and was dragging me to his waiting carriage.

I tried to pull away, but I was weak and this man was strong, even for his age. The coachman took no notice of my screams or my pleas for help; they went unheeded, both by him and by my father's own servants.

Mr Carter lifted me up and pushed me inside, then climbed in beside me and slammed the door shut. I could still hear my mother's screams but I was unsure whether she was crying for me or from the beating my father was giving her.

I tried to push myself as far into the corner of the seat as I could while the man ordered his coachman to drive on. Then he turned to me and smiled; it was not a welcoming, friendly smile, but one I could not interpret. Now I know it was a smile of lust, but then I had never before seen any such smile directed at me.

"Your father told no lie," Mr Carter said. "You are beautiful. Even more beautiful up close than when I first saw you in the street. You will be the most beautiful little girl we have ever entertained."

I had been told before that I was beautiful, and I had always been quite pleased. I had no way of knowing that those same words coming from this man would warp my emotions every time I heard them for the rest of my life.

Mr Carter's coachman returned me to my father's house late that night. He had to climb down and carry me inside because I could not walk and I cannot remember when I have ever been in so much pain. I remember him handing me over to a manservant of my father's who carried me upstairs to my bedchamber, and every step he took brought further agony.

I have tried all my life to blot out the events of that long and painful day, tried to forget Mr Carter and his friend who took turns to rape me, then thought themselves generous when they produced a sumptuous meal at midday and were angry that I could not eat. The friend had a long and deep T shaped scar down the side of his face that made him look like a monster out of a fairy tale. He had a skinny body that made his head look too big, and that made him even more of an ogre to my ten year old imagination. That scar imprinted itself on my nightmares for many years to come.

I am talking now from the perspective of an experienced woman, not the child I was. I did not know what was happening, only that it hurt badly and that it was wrong and embarrassing. That was not the way I should have learned that men are built differently from women, but that was my father's special birthday present.

The more I struggled, the more the two men laughed at my helplessness and I overheard them telling each other that I had been worth every penny that I had cost.

I was terrified by this talk, as it seemed to me that my father must have sold me to them and that I would have to spend all my days like this one. Despite the terrible pain I was in, I was so relieved to be delivered back to my home, I was sobbing with it.

I had no nurse or governess. I had once, but that was before my father had squandered all his money and could afford such a thing. Any education or care that I received was from my mother and that night she was there at my bedside, carefully removing what was left of my clothing.

She moved slowly and I knew even at that age that it was because she was also in pain. She moved with one arm held to her ribs, the other being the only one she could use. I had witnessed this before; it was nothing new. Her bruises were angry and her eye was swollen shut, yet still she tended to my wounds that were bleeding heavily.

"Enough is enough," she said quietly. "I thought I could not suffer any more at his hands, but what he has done this day has been too much. Tomorrow we leave."

I sat up as best I could and leaned against the pillows.

"Leave?" I asked. "Where will we go? We have nowhere to go, do we?"

"We will go to my brother," she replied regretfully.

"Your brother? I did not know you had a brother."

"We have not spoken for many years," she said quietly. "Not since long before I married. My father turned him out; he did not approve of the woman he married and would have nothing more to do with him. But my father died before he had time to change his will, so Stephen still inherited the bulk of his fortune."

"But you know where he is?" I asked.

She nodded.

"He inherited my father's house, the one I grew up in. I assume he is still there, at least I pray so. Sleep now," she said, putting her hand gently on my forehead. "We will leave in the morning and go to London to find your uncle."

I slept fitfully for a few short hours, my dreams filled with images from the day. I relived every horrifying moment and when I woke in the dark, cold room, I forced myself to stay awake, wondering if I would ever sleep again.

I was also concerned about how we would escape the house without my father stopping us. I could not bear the thought of my mother receiving another severe beating at his hands and I wished I were grown up and able to defend her. She was too weak now; I did not think she would survive.

I need not have worried as the next day there was no sign of my father. I had no idea where he could be, as his usual habit was to start drinking before breakfast. It was unlikely that he would have gone out riding or even walking, and besides it was pouring with rain. He was a man who liked his comforts.

When I asked my mother she only told me that we were in luck and to hurry before he came back. I needed no more prompting than that.

***

I remember little about the journey to London except that I was terrified every time we had to stop that my father would appear out of nowhere and order us home.

The carriage was damp and cold and we kept the blinds down to keep out the rain. Every bump in the road broad me fresh agony and I cuddle against my mother for comfort. It was my father's carriage and we were driven by his own coachman; I remember being surprised about this and that my mother handed over her emerald necklace to him before we boarded the coach. I realise now that was his payment for taking us and for keeping quiet about it but then I was just scared that he would tell.

By the time we arrived at my uncle's house, I was in a lot more pain from the day before and I noticed that my mother was having difficulty breathing. It took her a long time to climb down from the carriage, each step was agony and left her with even less breath.

She stood still and looked up at the house before carefully moving forward.

"This is where I grew up," she said softly. "This was my father's house."

I did not reply as I was only surprised that she was telling me this much. She never normally spoke about her past or anything that had led to her marriage to my father, who was many years older than her.

I know now that she was forced into a marriage with him because he was titled and her family were wealthy commoners. There was nothing unusual about this arrangement, that an impoverished aristocrat would trade his title for a rich dowry and all a woman could do was pray for a kind man. My mother's prayers had gone unheeded.

My uncle did not seem pleased to see his sister after so many years. When first he opened the door he just stood and stared at us, as though he had no idea who we were. My mother was leaning against the porch pillar, unable to stand without support, and I wanted to scream at him to let us in. Even a stranger would have let us in, seeing the state of us. He took us in at last, gave us refreshments and when he realised how bad was our condition, sent for a physician.

My uncle assigned us bedchambers, just in time as it happens. My mother collapsed in the hallway outside and he scooped her up in his arms and laid her on the bed.

"Stay with her," Uncle Stephen told me. "I have no idea what has happened to you two, but it does not look good. She can hardly breathe and you are having difficulty walking. And there is blood on your skirt."

I felt myself blushing a deep red and my cheeks grew hot and uncomfortable. Why did he have to say that, even if it were true? I fled from the room and into the chamber he had given to me.

"Forgive me," he said following me. "I did not mean to cause you any distress, but I do need to know what has happened. I need to be able to tell the physician when he arrives."

I just hid under the covers and shook my head furiously.

The physician arrived shortly after and examined my mother first, then came in to me. You would have thought that after my ordeal I would find nothing else embarrassing, but this man prodding and poking was excruciatingly shaming as well as painful. And I was sure I had done something for which I was to blame, I was sure that either my uncle or the doctor would shout at me, tell me I had been wicked.

He did not speak to me, not even to ask what had happened, but just shook his head mournfully and returned to the adjoining room where my mother lie unconscious.

I had crept out of bed with great difficulty and was listening from the adjoining chamber.

"I am sorry, Mr Jameson," he told my uncle. "I do not believe that your sister will live. She is bleeding internally and there is nothing I can do."

I felt the tears spill out over my face. My mother was going to die and I would have no one. What would happen to me? Uncle Stephen would have to send me back to my father, would he not? Then what would happen when he ran out of money? What would happen when he lost his temper and had no one else on whom to use his whip.

I suddenly felt that Mother was the lucky one. I would certainly rather be dead than return to my father.

"Try whatever you can," Uncle Stephen was telling the doctor. "What of my niece?"

"Your little niece has been horrifically abused, Sir," the physician said in a shocked voice. "I have never in my life seen anything like it. Indeed, I am deeply shocked."

"Abused?" Uncle Stephen asked with a frown. "What does that mean exactly? What sort of abuse? My sister has been abused, that is obvious."

"Your sister, Sir, has been badly beaten but the little girl has been raped, repeatedly I would say. She has extensive injuries, bruises and tearing, that will likely heal up partially, if not completely, but I have to tell you that the chances of her ever being a mother are very remote."

Raped? That was the first time in my life I had heard that word and I had no real idea of what it meant even then.

The doctor stopped talking then rubbed his chin reflectively. "How did this happen, Sir?"

Uncle Stephen looked outraged.

"I wish I knew," he replied. "They arrived this morning. I have not seen my sister in many years and my niece not at all. This is obviously why they were running away."

"He sold me," I said in a shaky voice from the doorway, causing both men to turn around and look at me.

"Sold you?" Uncle Stephen asked. "Who? Who would do such a thing?"

"My father," I replied, realising that I had at last summoned up the courage to speak of it. "He took one thousand pieces of gold from a man and that man took me away and kept me all day yesterday. He and his friend. There was something said about clearing his debts as well."

That was the first glimmer of pity or compassion I had seen from my uncle. He had obviously not wanted to receive us into his household, but now he stepped forward and gathered me into his arms. I flinched, from pain and from fear. I did not want him to touch me.

"Forgive me, little one," he said quietly releasing his hold. "You can stay here as long as you wish, you and your mother."

"Not my mother," I replied. "She is dying. Will you send me back to my father?"

"No!" My uncle cried out at once. "Whatever it costs me, you will never have to see him again. I promise you."

I retreated into my bedchamber then and climbed under the covers to weep for my lost mother and for my lost innocence.

CHAPTER TWO

Uncle Stephen was a widower. My grandfather had no need to disown him, since the woman he had taken to wife had died in childbirth shortly after their marriage, along with his only child. He had never remarried and he never wanted another child, deeming them to be too much heartache. I suppose that me turning up in that state just proved him right.

My mother died later that day and for a while I was afraid that Uncle Stephen would send me back to my father, despite his earlier promise, but nothing was said about it. Being a child, nobody bothered to tell me anything and all I found out was from listening at doors, a habit I carried with me into adulthood. I learned that way that my father had disappeared, that his house and lands which had cost me so dear were now in the possession of Mr Carter and his friend.

Now I believe that the man had somehow tricked my drunken father into signing over his entire estate as well as his daughter. I believed they had murdered him, and that my mother had known and done nothing. She was certainly not surprised at his absence on the morning we left. But I could not care. Uncle Stephen said I could stay with him and that was all I could have wanted. He was a kind enough man, though no special favours were ever given. He was obviously only doing his duty by having me there and had no special affection for me. He was anxious that I should have a governess to keep me to my place either in the schoolroom or in my own chamber.

London was exciting after my years in the countryside and even without leaving the house, there was always something to see from my window. There were men and women selling things, fruit, vegetables, milk, meat. There was one young woman I saw every single night who did not seem to be selling anything, but she would disappear into an alleyway with a man sometimes. Of course, I know now what she was selling, that same thing that had been brutally torn from me.

I felt safe with Uncle Stephen, safe for the first time in my life and I began to trust him as time raced by.

We settled into an uneasy friendship, only speaking when necessary, never talking about my ordeal. I would have liked someone to talk to, but not about that really. As I grew older, the normal bodily functions of puberty came sporadically and hurt when they did. It was my governess who told me what it was, but she of course did not know why I suffered so much more than most young girls. I would have died of shame had she found out.

***

It had been three years since my mother and I had arrived on Uncle Stephen's doorstep, she at the point of death, me not much better, and I was grateful to him for giving me a home even though he had not really wanted me.

It was an anxious time in London. The King had abandoned his lawful wife, Queen Katherine, and was trying to persuade the pope to grant him a divorce so that he could remarry. Tensions ran high and I was warned not to repeat any gossip that I might hear, but my uncle was not close to the court and although I was the daughter of an Earl, I had no wish to go there and had no one to present me in any case.

I did not know then that Uncle Stephen could have paid a member of the nobility to take me in and present me at court, and I am not sure whether he knew that himself or whether he felt under an obligation to keep me safe with him. I hoped it was the latter and in any case, I was quite happy with the arrangement. The King and all his courtiers held no attraction for me, despite the beautiful clothes and jewels they wore.

My uncle and I attended mass each week, along with our servants, and one day after the service the priest informed us that the King had established himself as the head of the church in

England, that we were no longer Roman Catholics, but English Catholics.

My uncle said nothing as we left the church, but when we arrived back at his house he warned me very seriously that I should forget the Pope in Rome had ever existed, that mentioning him at all could anger the King and be extremely dangerous.

I shivered at his warning. I had seen the King, had seen that tiny mouth and those angry eyes; I had no wish to be on the wrong end of his wrath.

Not long after that there were parades in London as the King married the Lady Anne Boleyn. Uncle Stephen took me out to watch the coronation parade when she was crowned Queen, but it was very frightening.

There were cries of "Long live Queen Katherine" and Anne's appearance caused much booing from the crowd. Nobody cheered, nobody wanted her and the King looked murderously angry. I felt a little sorry for Lady Anne Boleyn that day, even though my uncle and I had not sympathised before. From what I had heard, she had manipulated the King into putting away his wife and making her Queen, when he had wanted only another mistress like all the others.

From the romantic ideals of a thirteen year old, I believed that she must have really loved him and he her, but I realise now that it was only lust, just like the two men who had destroyed my life. My view of men was already one of suspicion, even before that parade when I attracted many glances.

Although I bore the title of Lady Rachel Stewart in my own right, Uncle Stephen had no such aristocratic claims which put me in an unusual and awkward position as I grew older. He wanted to find a titled gentleman for me to marry, but it would be difficult when he had no access to the court in his own right.

By this time I had found out, again through listening to servants' gossip, that what was done to me was normal for married couples. I did not know that it was the act without the brutality, but even if I had done, I would not have understood why anyone would want to get married and suffer so.

When Uncle Stephen first put the idea of a marriage to me, I was horrified.

"No, Uncle," I told him. "You have no need to concern yourself about finding a titled gentlemen, since I shall not be marrying anyone."

He grinned slightly.

"So you think I am going to keep you for the rest of your life?"

"I can find something to do, surely. Perhaps I can be a governess when I am older, like Mistress Browning is to me."

"That would hardly be a fitting position for a lady of the nobility, for an Earl's daughter," he argued.

"What then? There must be something I can do. What do other ladies in my position do?"

"They marry," he answered. "That is what they do. Never mind, we will talk about it when you are a little older perhaps."

"We have no need to talk about it at all," I said determinedly.

What I had not noticed on the day of the coronation, that my uncle had, was how many gentlemen turned their heads to look at me. Even the King, so I was told later, paid particular attention to me, standing beside the road and watching the carriages with everyone else.

It was but two weeks later that my uncle received an offer for my hand in marriage from a wealthy, titled gentleman, the Earl of Connaught.

I was not consulted, and Uncle Stephen was very pleased with this offer, but I was terrified. It had never occurred to me that I might be chosen to marry anyone, since I had no dowry and no titled relations to assist. When we had spoken about it before, I imagined Uncle Stephen having to go out of his way to find someone willing to marry me, someone with a title. This offer was unexpected and very unwelcome.

"I cannot marry," I told him in a panic. "I am just thirteen years old."

"It is old enough, beyond the age of consent."

I was shocked and talk of marriage brought back those memories that I had tried very hard to put away forever. Surely my uncle must understand how I would feel about a marriage to anyone. I would rather take the veil, but that was not possible since the King was dissolving all the monasteries and convents.

"You cannot have forgotten what was done to me, Uncle," I replied pleadingly "and it still hurts."

I blushed and he frowned a little, then shrugged as though he thought I was inventing excuses.

"No, I have not and I have explained to the Earl that you are no virgin. He seemed to sympathise."

I just stared at him, hardly able to believe my ears.

"You told a stranger all about it? How dare you!"

"He is offering you marriage, Rachel, a good marriage. This is not an opportunity we can overlook; it will not come a second time."

"Does he know that I cannot give him children?" I demanded, suddenly recalling what I had overheard the physician telling my uncle. He looked startled that I knew. He did not know that I had overheard the physician talking to him and I had never mentioned it. It was unimportant; I was not going to marry, was I? I was not concerned that I might be barren.

"No. It is not certain that you are barren, is it? The doctor did not know for certain so it might be wise to keep quiet on that score."

I could scarcely believe what I was hearing. Uncle Stephen had not ill treated me but he was apparently more anxious to get rid of me than I had suspected. I had tried so hard to keep out of his way, to leave him to his solitude; there was no real need for him to be so eager for me to go.

"Supposing I tell him myself?"

"Then you will no longer be welcome in my house," he replied firmly. "This man noticed you in the crowd and wants to marry you. He is an Earl, so the same rank as your father and I see no other way I m going to find you someone so illustrious."

"I know nothing about him," I replied frantically. "Who is he? What age is he? Is he widowed or unmarried? You cannot just marry me to a stranger; I am supposed to give my consent. Even I know that much."

"You can refuse your consent if you wish," he replied quietly. "But if you do you will leave this house immediately. I do not believe you have anywhere else to go, which should make the prospect of this marriage more appealing to you. He is thirty years of age I believe. His first wife died ten years ago and he has mourned her ever since. It seems it was a love match, so you are lucky to have attracted his attention. I believe he does not want another love match, merely an ornament to hang off his arm and entertain his guests. You are very, very beautiful. I do not believe you realise that, which modesty makes you even more appealing."

That was the first time I had felt that horror when someone told me I was beautiful; it would not be the last. All I could think of was sitting in that carriage with Mr Carter, of shrinking back into the corner while he told me I was beautiful, the most beautiful little girl he had ever entertained.

***

So I was to be married to the Earl of Connaught, a man almost twenty years older than me and about whom I knew nothing. It seemed that my very existence was merely for the convenience of various men and I wondered if this one would prove to be another deviant who wanted to abuse me and share me with his friends.

I tried to run away. I stole some jewellery from my uncle's bedchamber, a necklace and bracelets that had belonged to his late wife, and I crept out of the house early one morning with them. I found a jeweller on the other side of the city, where I thought no one would know me, and asked him to buy them, but he recognised me from the coronation parade. He had seen me there with my uncle and he knew my uncle, so he kept me there while he sent for him.

"After everything I have done for you," Uncle Stephen said angrily, grabbing my upper arm and pushing me along the pavement. "You steal from me? And my dear wife's jewels as well. I cannot believe it."

"Then perhaps the fact that I did that will make you understand how desperate I am. I cannot be married."

He just looked down at me and shook his head slowly.

"It will be all right," he said. "It will not be like your ordeal, I promise."

He did not understand. No man could really understand, no matter how hard he tried. I felt sick to my stomach at the very idea.

***

The marriage took place at St Paul's Cathedral, which made my uncle very proud. He told me that he felt happier now that he had found a proper place for me, as he had no idea how to go about finding a suitable match. He blessed the day he took me to the coronation parade, while I cursed that day and wished it had never happened.

It was all King Henry's fault. If he had stayed married to his lawful wife, there would have been no coronation parade, no Queen Anne, no Earl of Connaught.

I could not make my uncle understand or even sympathise. He seemed to think it was the normal sort of nervous behaviour of a bride to be and for that I would never forgive him.

His Lordship did not wish to meet me before the ceremony, did not wish to learn about me or find out if he even liked me. It seemed that his only interest was in how I looked, and people kept telling me I looked beautiful. They could not know how those words made me cringe. I did not feel beautiful and after my tenth birthday ordeal, I doubted that I ever would.

He was a reasonably personable gentleman, a little stout perhaps but had he been skinny he would have resembled that other one too much for comfort. He had blondish hair and blue eyes, and a slightly pimply complexion.

I resented the way I had been forced into this marriage, but I decided to try to be a good wife, since it was obviously my fate to be the Countess of Connaught. There could well be compensations though I was really too young to consider what they might be.

The first time we met was in the church where we stood through a long and complicated wedding mass, pledging our lives to one another. He did not speak to me at all, not until that night when the servants came along to take me to his bedchamber, to wash me and undress me and put me into the bed to await his pleasure.

That is when panic set in and the memories came flooding back. I closed my eyes and could see again that horrible T shaped scar and hear the laughter. There would be no pleasure in this night for me, that was for certain.

When he eventually decided to join me, after a wait of some half hour during which I had fallen asleep, he removed his clothing, climbed into the bed, rubbed himself until he was ready then shoved himself into me, telling me to lie still. Then he left, leaving me to feel the pain all over again.

It was not long before the reason became apparent. He wanted an heir and it was believed that a woman should lie still to ensure a secure pregnancy. I did not tell him that I was probably not capable of conceiving. I might have, had he treated me with any sort of respect, but I did not think that he deserved it. I did not know then that had I told him, I would have been given some peace, he would have had no further interest in me. I thought I was taking revenge, but all I was doing was prolonging the agony.

I was married to a man who did not speak to me, did not do anything for me except to make sure I was dressed in accordance with his rank. My clothing was always beautiful and expensive, velvets and satins, cloth of silver, all in shades that went well with my dark hair.

He presented me at court, but only because it was expected, while for my part I hated every minute spent there. I felt shy and inadequate and had nothing to say. The Earl ignored me for the rest of the time, but every night he performed his disgusting and painful ritual, every month he looked for signs of a pregnancy I knew would not happen. The knowledge gave me a sense of satisfaction, a feeling of power over him.

When the King called for his courtiers to sign the Act of Supremacy, supporting his claim to be the head of the church, His Lordship signed without hesitation. I presumed that religion meant little to him and he was not about to risk his life for it, unlike Sir Thomas More who faced the executioner rather than deny his beliefs.

Many people mourned Sir Thomas. I had seen him once, at court. He was much loved and had a family, a wife, a son and daughters who cared more for him than for the King. His head went missing from its spike on London Bridge and it was rumoured that it was his daughter, Margaret Roper who had climbed up there during the night and taken it.

The Earl took me to court on a number of occasions, for various balls and celebrations that the King gave and I could not help but notice that men looked at me, took more notice of me than most of the women there. I could also not help but notice the smug look of satisfaction that those glances gave to the Earl. He was very pleased that his wife was considered such a lovely creature, while I would rather have disappeared into the floor and let some other woman have their attention.

I also noticed that the King himself gave me more than a passing glance or that his Queen treated me to one of her disdainful, angry looks. I would really rather not attend any of these functions, but I had no choice. Even once when I feigned illness, I was still made to go.

I had been married to the Earl for a year or so when I decided that it was time I established myself as a person, even though I did not have the confidence for the task. Surely it must have occurred to him by now that there would be no child, so why did he bother to perform his ritual every night? I could not believe that he enjoyed it any more than I did myself. I doubt it caused him any pain though, which it did me. I did not know then that it was not painful for every woman, that it was my own special burden. I only wondered why God had made women so weak that they felt pain every time and thought perhaps it was to be sure of their chastity.

"My Lord," I said one night when he had finished with me. "Can I ask a question?"

He had climbed out of the bed, as always, to return to his own chamber and now he looked down at me as though he had not realised that I could actually talk. He nodded his consent.

"What will happen if by some strange chance I should conceive a son? Will he also be taught that I am not worth talking to?"

He frowned a puzzled frown, as though not quite sure of my meaning.

"It seems unlikely to happen does it not, so the question is irrelevant. I do not understand it anyway."

"My uncle told you that I was not a virgin?"

"He did," he replied stiffly. "At the time I believed it would make the physical side easier, you being so young. But it seems not to be the case as I still find it difficult."

I laughed then, I could not help it. Perhaps things would not be quite so 'difficult' if he bothered to treat me with any sort of affection. I was not about to reveal that it was 'difficult' because it hurt me so much. I would not ask for sympathy when I expected none. But a frown of anger crossed his brow; perhaps he thought I was laughing at him, and perhaps I was.

"Was your first wife treated the same as me?" I asked him boldly.

"You will not speak of her," he replied angrily, raising his voice.

I felt angry then and determined to wield a little power of my own.

"Did my uncle happen to mention how I lost my virginity? Did it not occur to you that it was uncommon in one so young?"

He started to shake his head slowly and I could see by his expression that he was not looking forward to what I had to say.

"He told me you were assaulted, yes," he said slowly.

"I was raped, Sir, repeatedly," I said firmly, "when I was a child. The physician told my uncle then that it was unlikely I would ever conceive."

His eyes widened in shock and fury, then he bent down and struck me across the face.

"Why did you not tell me yourself?" He demanded angrily.

"It did not occur to me that you would want me to tell you anything, Sir," I replied with a little smirk. I was glad he was angry, glad that I had demolished his little idea of having an heir. Perhaps now he would leave me alone at night.

I know my expression made him even angrier and he grabbed my shoulders and started to shake me, until I thought my neck would break. Still I was not afraid. It seemed to me then that if he killed me, I would find a place in heaven and put an end to all the horror of this life. Purgatory could be no worse than this. After another hard slap he dropped me back on to the bed and marched out of the room. I never saw him again.

The Earl left the house the next morning and never returned. I had a visit from a lawyer, wanting to know the details of my marriage. It seemed that my husband was trying to find a way to get himself a divorce, but that was one thing he could not buy. The King had managed to get one; perhaps he thought himself as important as the King.

I was fifteen when I became a widow for the first time, when word reached me that the Earl had died after a fall from his horse. I felt nothing except a little concern that the King might marry me off to someone else, someone who had some other use for me.

I had thought at least that now I would not have to depend upon a man to survive, that the Earl would have left his fortune and house to me, but even in that I was mistaken. It seemed that he had left the bulk of his fortune to a distant cousin and the house would also go to him when I no longer needed it to live in. So, even in death he was punishing me because of my uncle's deception.

It was not long after his death that suitors began calling. I have no idea how they knew about me or where I lived, but it seemed that word had got around court circles that the very beautiful Countess of Connaught was in need of a new husband.

The first one to call took me by surprise as I had not expected it. The servant showed him in, announced him as the Marquis of Davenport and brought refreshments. He was about forty years old with greying hair and many wrinkles. He also had a bulging abdomen that stuck out beneath his doublet and a double chin.

I was still naive, despite my experiences, and had no real idea of what he wanted.

"My Lady," he said at once, taking my hand and kissing it. I could not avoid stiffening somewhat at his touch and I know he must have noticed it but he chose to ignore it and kept hold of my hand. "It is true what they have been saying; you are very beautiful."

Once more those words transported me back to a dark carriage and a leering stranger. I pulled my hand away and indicated a seat, as far away from mine as possible.

"I have come to offer my services, My Lady," he began. "I realise that you are recently widowed but enquiries have revealed that you have no male relative on whom you can depend to help you through this sad time."

"I have an uncle, Sir," I replied.

"So I have heard, but he cannot escort you to the palace and I have heard you have no one else. I was hoping we might become friends."

"I have no need nor desire to go to the palace," I told him.

He smiled benignly. "You say that now, my dear, but you will soon miss the gaiety and the excitement."

As always, nobody was interested in my wishes, only their own.

"Who sent you, Sir?" I demanded, feeling the tears spring to my eyes. "Who told you I might be in need of your services?"

I asked the question because I was sure it was Uncle Stephen, meddling in my life again, trying to find me another title to marry. I was shocked by the Marquis' reply.

"His Majesty the King asked me to come," he replied proudly.

"The King? Why?"

"My wife died a few months ago and His Majesty was kind enough to think of you as a possible match. I know you are recently widowed and it is too early to think of such things, but I thought it best to introduce myself before some other fellow snapped you up."

I could scarcely believe my ears. Was I to spend all my life at the beck and call of every man whose attention I caught? I stood quickly and went to the door, where I called for Alice, my senior maidservant.

"You will leave, please Sir," I told the Marquis. "You may thank His Majesty for his concern, but inform him that I have no intention of marrying again, ever."

He shook his head slowly and smiled, a smile that told me he did not take me seriously, that I was in mourning and would soon come round to his way of thinking.

Of course, my wishes were of no importance to anyone. More titled gentlemen appeared at my door, some young, some old, but all with those same words on their lips: "You are very beautiful," and that same lascivious look in their eyes.

Not a single one of them seemed to notice how I hated to hear that; perhaps they all believed it was modesty that made me cringe away from them, made me stiffen when they touched my hand.

Eventually, I told the servants to refuse admittance to anyone. I cared nothing for custom, I cared not that it might be uncivil. I just wanted to be left alone.

**

I had heard rumours that the King's marriage to Queen Anne was not all he had wanted, that she had failed to give him a son just like Queen Katherine and that he spent little time with her now. I heard from servants' gossip that he had returned to his mistresses, but it was just of passing interest to me. What King Henry did was of no concern of mine, so long as he forgot my existence and left me in peace.

I was denied my wish. Only a few weeks after the death of my husband, the King sent for me to attend him late at night.

CHAPTER THREE

My first reaction was to refuse, but I knew that would never be allowed. There was a servant from the palace standing in my bedchamber and waiting for me to give him an answer, but why I could not imagine since there was only one answer that would be accepted.

I had heard that this was what happened when a woman had attracted the King. I had also heard that Queen Anne had refused the king's attention and that had resulted in his interest growing. But she had been the niece of the Duke of Norfolk, a much more important lady than I. That is how she became Queen.

Better to accept my fate, as I had accepted my fate on many occasions, than to tread such a dangerous path as her. I had no desire to be Queen, or mistress, but if they were my choices I would choose the latter. A far safer option I would have thought.

So I dressed and followed the palace servant to his waiting coach. Inside the King's chamber my heart began to hammer loudly. I had hoped that when my husband had died I would be left in peace, that I would be allowed to hide away in his London house and not attract the attention of any man. This beauty that they all said I had was a cruel curse and no mistake. Sometimes I felt like slashing my face with a knife, so that no man would ever want me again. If only I had the courage!

This man who approached me was old by my standards, but I had been subjected to old men before. He was a big man though, heavily built, with striking red hair and an easy smile on his tiny mouth. I felt that there was more behind that smile though, as it did not reach his eyes and that he was so used to getting his own way, his anger would be dreadful if he were refused anything. Queen Anne must be a braver woman than I. There were rumours that he was a great lover, although I was really not sure what they meant. What did a man have to do to be a great lover?

He was holding out his hand to me, waiting for me to take it, and I cursed the tears that began to gather as I gave him a deep curtsey before taking that hand. I was shaking, my heart hammering, my legs trembling.

"My dear," he said. "Do not be afraid. You are so very beautiful, it would be a shame to spoil such beauty with tears would it not?"

Those words again; and they sounded no better coming from royal lips.

"Yes, your majesty," I replied, not knowing what else to say.

"Come, sit beside me and tell me all about yourself," the King said gently, leading me to a settle before the fire.

Tell him about myself? Why, I thought, would he want to know? I could not remember a time in my life when any man had wanted me to say anything, so why would this illustrious one wish to know? Of course, he did not really have any interest in my life; it was just a rouse to get me to relax and he would never remember what I told him in the morning.

"There is nothing to say, your majesty," I replied.

I could think of nothing else to say. I had not had the practice at conversation that another woman might have had and I hoped that this flaw in my character might make him leave me alone, but it was not to be.

"That is all right," he replied. "I like a woman who is mysterious."

Then he leaned toward me and kissed my lips. I had never been kissed by a man before, never, and it was an odd experience. His lips were wet and his breath stank, and I wanted to wipe my mouth on my sleeve but dare not. I knew there were worse things to come so was unsurprised when his hand started to crawl up my skirts. I tried to curl myself into an imaginary ball, but it did not work, did not make him realise how I hated his hands on me or if it did, he did not care. His only interest, like all men, was what he wanted.

He took my hand again and led me to the bed, where he started to remove my clothing. I had not experienced this before; I had always had to be waiting in the bed, already naked. I found the experience embarrassing in the extreme, reminding me bitterly of my tenth birthday. I started to cry again, but it did not seem to have much affect.

"I think you being so shy is charming," he said softly. "Such a refreshing change."

So there would be no escape no matter what I did. Once I stood naked before him he lifted me into his arms and placed me in the bed. He took off his own clothes then and climbed in beside me, then he began to run his hands over my breast and thighs. Once more I was ten years old and helpless, once more I was in pain and terror. I began to sob but it did not stop him, not till he had finished with me while I just lie still as I had been taught.

He said nothing else, merely left me to get dressed. A servant came in to help lace my bodice then I was taken back to the waiting coach and delivered back to the house. Once there, I climbed into bed and cried myself to sleep, wondering if there were any life for me, wondering why God had chosen to make me look like this if all it brought was heartache.

It seemed that I had disappointed the King as he did not send for me a second time and for that I was grateful. I had little to do with my time, my late husband having left a pension for me as long as I stayed unmarried, which would be a lifetime if I had my way.

I rarely left the house. Wherever I went I attracted the stares of both men and women, men with a lecherous leer and women with a haughty vindictiveness which hurt even more. I felt happier just staying at home. I had no wish to go to court, no wish to attract the further attention of the King, nor the jealousy of his Queen who was no longer in favour. He had got rid of one Queen so why not this one too?

But he had no excuse to divorce Anne, there was no saying that it was not a valid marriage as he had done with Queen Katherine. I had a feeling she would not go quietly, but in the meantime the servants' gossip told me that the King was already pursuing another.

I only found out what was going on by listening at doors. Since the only person in my life who had ever talked to me and listened to me was my mother, and since she had been dead now for almost six years, it is what I had become accustomed to. It never occurred to me to actually ask anybody, even the servants.

I remember the day of Queen Anne's execution as vividly as I recall my tenth birthday. I would not have believed it possible that someone who had caused such a major upheaval as a change of religion in the land, could be brought to nothing at the whim of one man.

She had been convicted of many crimes, witchcraft, adultery, even incest with her own brother, and now she would face the executioner. I was not alone in believing that her only crime had been ambition, had been in thinking she could oust the rightful Queen and take her place. Her avarice had been her downfall. It was said a swordsman had been sent from France to cut off her head, as a concession to the love the King had once had for her. If that was love, I could well live without it. I was very glad I had disappointed the King and not become his next great attraction.

CHAPTER FOUR

I was seventeen before anyone remembered my existence again and for that I was grateful. I had spent those two years alone except for the servants, who were paid under the terms of my late husband's will, but they did not speak unless spoken to and I had nothing to say. I was certain that at least one of them was stealing from me, but I did not have the courage to confront her.

I had no one to talk to, but that was what I preferred. I had my books into which I could disappear, and even had there been anyone, I would not have had anything to say. What could someone like me say to anyone? My only experiences of life were not something I wanted to speak of.

I had become a recluse and rarely left the house. The King's marriage to Jane Seymour had produced a much wanted heir and it was the celebration of the prince's birth that brought an invitation to court and it was not one I could refuse.

I was very much afraid that now that I was older, I might once more attract the King's attention should I show myself at court, even though it was said that he was much devoted to Queen Jane. I had no male protector to accompany me, either, which was not a normal state of affairs. I had no idea if I was supposed to go alone or bring one of the manservants with me. My uncle could not be presented, as he was a commoner, but I decided it was high time I paid him a visit anyway.

I had not seen him since my marriage to the Earl of Connaught and I had no wish to ever see him again, but for what I had in mind it was necessary.

He looked up from his paperwork when a maidservant let me in to his private rooms, but he could not even muster a smile for me.

"Rachel," he said. "Or should I say, Your Ladyship? What are you doing here?"

"I need money," I replied at once. I had no experience of building up to things, of explaining myself or making small talk. "I want to take the veil and there are no institutions left in England. I want to go to France, but I do not have the funds."

He frowned at me for a moment then shrugged.

"No," he said.

I was taken aback. I know not why I expected him to simply hand over the necessary funds, but it seemed that it would be to his advantage as well as mine. Sealed up behind convent walls, he would have no further need to think about me at all. I had not anticipated an argument.

"Why? You have no need of me. What difference does it make to you?"

"You have your husband's pension and his house. If you leave, you will lose that and when you decide to return there will be nowhere for you to go."

"Return? Why would I want to return?"

"You are young," he replied. "You have no idea to what you are committing yourself. You will find another husband."

I was shaking my head, the idea sending a shudder through me.

"No!" I cried, raising my voice a little in panic. It occurred to me then for the first time that my uncle might take this request as an invitation to find me another husband, but I hoped I was wrong. He had no access to the court, but that had not stopped him before. "I have no wish to remarry, Uncle. I only want to take the veil, to be somewhere quiet where I am not obliged to be with any man."

"The idea of all that beauty shut away behind convent walls is barbaric," he said. "I am your guardian and I will not allow it."

"You will allow me to be used though, will you not? You will allow me to be taken advantage of by disgusting old men, and paraded around like a lovely doll. You will allow me to prostitute myself to the King of England, to be sent for to share his bed like any common whore off the streets!"

I realised that was the absolute longest speech I had ever given in my life and wondered where the words had come from. Perhaps they had been building up for so long that they came out of their own accord.

My uncle did not look shocked, just pleased. A little smile started to form on his lips.

"The King? The King has sent for you to lie with him?"

"A long time ago, yes."

"Just once?" He sounded disappointed at that. "What did you do to disappoint him? You could have asked favours, titles."

Titles for himself he meant.

"I did nothing, just as I had been taught. Lie still and suffer for their pleasure." He flinched then, but said no more. "Would you perhaps have me deceive the King into believing that I might produce a son, just as you deceived Lord Connaught?"

He sighed and shook his head.

"I will not allow you passage to France," he said at last. "It is not what my sister would have wanted."

"What do you care? How do you know what my mother might have wanted? You did not even know her, did not bother to find out about her suffering."

"The King has dissolved all the abbey lands. It would not be a good reflection on our family if you were to go to France to join one. It could be dangerous."

"For you, maybe. Not for me; I would be safe in France!"

I turned and fled the room in tears. This had been my only hope that I might not have to attend the baptism celebrations, that I would not be required to go to court and perhaps attract the attention of yet another lecherous man. Perhaps I could feign illness.

When I got home my manservant told me that I had a visitor.

"The Earl of Summerville is here to see you, My Lady," he said.

"The Earl of who?"

Of course he did not reply but took my cloak and turned away, while I stood and wondered what sort of man had been sent to meet me this time. I would not marry this one, no matter what the King said. I was supposed to consent to a marriage, that was the law, but what chance had I of refusing if the King ordered it? The punishment for disobeying would be great indeed.

While I stood I remembered the endless nights with Lord Connaught, my night with the King and the pain involved in both. I remembered my tenth birthday, and tears sprang to my eyes. I wanted desperately to turn and run from the house, but I had nowhere to go. I took a deep breath and steeled myself to walk into the chamber and meet this man, and discover what he wanted from me.

The man who quickly got to his feet when I appeared was not at all what I had been expecting. He was young for one thing, not much older than me, and pleasing to look upon with his dark hair and eyes.

He approached me and bowed over the hand I presented to him then he looked up quickly as I shrank away and immediately released me. He smiled then, and it was not a smile I had ever seen directed at me before, not a smile of lasciviousness nor of satisfaction, not even a smile of admiration. It was a smile of delighted pleasure, of real warmth.

"My Lady," he said gently. "His Majesty has asked me to present myself to you as a possible escort to the celebrations for the Prince's birth. I am told you have no male relative to accompany you."

"That is kind of you, My Lord," I replied nervously.

"Not kind at all," he insisted. "My wife is unable to attend and I am only too happy to assist a beautiful woman."

I stiffened as the words 'beautiful woman' brought a cold scowl to my expression and I know that he noticed it.

"I trust it is nothing serious," I said, "that is keeping Lady Summerville from attending herself."

He studied me for a few moments before he replied.

"Not serious, no," he said, "but likely incurable."

I hardly knew what to say to that. How an illness could be incurable but not serious was beyond me, and I was not about to ask.

"Can I offer you some refreshments, My Lord?" I asked, changing the subject.

"That would be welcome," he replied. "We can discuss the details for tomorrow night, assuming that my company will be acceptable to you."

"Of course, My Lord," I replied uncertainly. "I am grateful."

There was really not much to discuss, as it happens, just times and when his carriage would arrive for me. It seemed that he wanted an excuse to stay, but for the first time in my life I did not feel threatened by his interest, nor did I feel the need to hurry the meeting.

He was young, handsome and married. Despite his odd statement about his wife, I imagined him to be quite happy with her and not in need of anything else. He could afford to give his time to talk to me.

The following hour was the first time in my life that a man, or anyone else for that matter apart from my mother, had actually talked to me. It seemed that this man was interested in me, me as a person not as a plaything or breeding vessel. Even when the King asked about me, I could tell that he was not really listening, that he just wanted to get on with the business of bedding me.

This Earl asked about my family, about my late husband, he asked about me, what things I liked to do. I could scarcely find the words to reply. I could hardly tell him about my late husband, since I barely even knew his name, nor about my tastes since I did not really have any.

"I spend a lot of time reading, My Lord," I replied. "I am used to my own company."

"Perhaps we can change your mind about that," he said. "You are young. You should be enjoying life, not hiding away from it."

"I have seen little to enjoy so far, My Lord," I told him.

I wanted to say a lot more, to tell him that I did not feel safe outside the house, that each time I showed my face somebody thought they had the right to use me to their own ends, because I had no means of my own. It seemed to me that this man would understand, though I had no idea why I thought so. He was a complete stranger, after all.

The following evening he arrived in a huge black carriage bearing his family crest. I was very nervous, I have to admit. I had not set foot inside the palace since that disastrous night when I was 'honoured' to share the King's bed and just being there brought up memories I would rather forget.

But my companion was as charming as he was handsome and we danced and ate and talked together like old friends. Not once was there a hint of anything untoward, no false flattery or unnecessary compliments which I did not trust, and I found to my surprise that I was actually enjoying myself. As usual there were many admiring glances that came my way, but there were an equal amount of women intensely interested in my companion.

It was the early hours of the morning when he delivered me back to my house and I was quite sad to see the evening end. Somehow he had instilled a confidence in me that I had never had before and I determined that things would change, that I would no longer listen at doors nor allow the servants to treat me like a child. Perhaps I could even choose one of them to be my special maid and companion as I had heard other ladies do.

"May I call on you again, My Lady?" The Earl was saying as he bade me goodnight by kissing my hand, an action that for the first time did not repel me.

I felt deflated by those words. Was this it then? Was he going to propose some sort of liaison like all the others, spoil the impression I had formed about him?

"Why would you want to do that, My Lord?" I asked abruptly.

"Because I think you are in need of a friend," he replied with a gentle smile. "And I would very much like to offer my services for that position."

It was not what I expected to hear but I could not help but think there must be some ulterior motive behind his offer.

"Will Lady Summerville be accompanying you, My Lord?" I asked significantly, wanting him to know that I had not forgotten his married state.

He was thoughtful for a few moments before he finally replied with a heavy sigh.

"She will if you want her to," he replied, but his expression had changed to one of concern. "I can bring her, but she will have nothing to say."

"I do not understand you, Sir."

"Suffice it to say," he said, "that she does not enjoy my company."

I spoke without thinking.

"I cannot believe that to be true," I said then quickly regretted it. "Forgive me. That was forward and not my concern."

"No matter." He paused then and gazed at me thoughtfully for a moment. "If I do bring her here," he went on, "would you think it an awful liberty if I asked you a favour?"

"What favour?"

"Would you talk to her? Try to find out why she is so afraid of me." He looked a little embarrassed but he continued: "I have never hurt her; I never would. She will not tell me, and she will not tell my mother."

"Your mother?" I replied, again without thinking. "I am not surprised. No woman would want to talk about intimate things to her husband's mother."

How I knew that I could not have said. I could only imagine if Lord Connaught had had a mother how it would have been to discuss his habits with her, or even the fact that he would not speak to me.

Lord Summerville seemed satisfied with my reply, but I could not help but feel sympathy for him. He seemed sad suddenly, as though mention of his wife had exposed him, kept him from hiding his hurt beneath his charm. I had been subjected to the most selfish and brutal behaviour by men and here was one of that gender actually concerned that his wife should be happy. I had no idea that such a creature existed.

"I shall take my leave and let you rest. Think about what I asked, please. I would consider it a great service and one more thing; please do not allow yourself to be hidden away." He paused for a moment before he went on: "I realise that you do not wish to hear it, but you really are far too beautiful to hide yourself away."

He left then while I watched him climb into his carriage and wave goodbye to me. I waved back, feeling somewhat disorientated. This had been a night of firsts for me. That was the first time anyone had told me I was beautiful without making me feel uncomfortable. The Earl had stated it as a fact, not in an admiring way but as he might have said the sky was blue or the grass was green. It was a strange feeling.

And I thought hard and long about his odd request. He had given me a lot in that one evening, far more than he could ever even suspect, and I felt I owed him something in return. Perhaps I could bring myself to speak to Lady Summerville, to befriend her and learn what troubled her. I had little experience of the normal world, but I could try to do it for him.

I was half afraid that my new found confidence might desert me after sleeping, but I still felt it when I awoke and I decided to do what I should have done months ago. I knew that one of my servants was robbing me, one of the senior ones at that who my late husband had placed in a position of trust. I determined to speak to her that morning, before my courage fled.

"I wish to know, Alice," I said firmly when she brought my breakfast, "What you have done with my diamond bracelet."

"My Lady? Have you lost another piece of jewellery?"

"I have not. Nor have I lost any others." I found the anger then to carry on. I had been treated like a backward child long enough. "I know you have stolen from me. I do not want someone in my house whom I cannot trust with my possessions or my secrets."

I thought she might at least lower her gaze, look ashamed, ask forgiveness. She would have had I been a man or a woman with more power. As it was, I was a helpless creature with no money and no male protection except an uncle who was not allowed to go to the same places as I, and who did not care for me anyway.

She shrugged and put down the tray.

"You mean like the handsome secret who brought his carriage for you last night, My Lady?" She asked impertinently.

"Lord Summerville is not a secret," I replied angrily. "He was sent by the King himself to escort me to the ball."

There was a definite smirk on her round face which made me angry enough to strike her, but I managed to keep myself under control.

"He may not be a secret yet," she went on, "but give him time."

No 'My Lady' that time. The woman was getting bolder and more insolent.

"What does that mean exactly," I demanded.

"Let us just say that His Lordship has something of a reputation with the ladies," she replied with that same smirk. "I mean, look at him! He would not give me a second glance but if he did, I would not be the one to refuse him."

I was horrified, both by her implication and by her brazenness.

"You have a foul mind, mistress," I replied quickly, "and I will thank you to remove it and yourself from my house and from my employment. You have one hour to get your things together and leave, and I mean your things, not mine!"

"You cannot do that," she argued. "I am not employed by you. You do not pay my wages."

"My late husband did not employ you to steal from me and accuse me of adultery."

"Your late husband did not employ me at all! It is your uncle who pays for this house and the servants, your clothing and your sustenance." She took a deep breath and looked satisfied that she had shocked me.

"My uncle?" I replied, shaking my head. "No. You are wrong. The Earl left this house and pension for me during my lifetime."

"No, he left you nothing. He did not care if you starved on the streets. It is your uncle who bought the house at auction and keeps you."

"Get out!" I screamed. "Get out now, and do not return!"

I must have screamed very loudly because at that moment Harry, one of the men servants opened the door without knocking and appeared with a look of real concern.

"My Lady," he said quickly. "Is everything all right?"

"No, it is not. Can you make sure that this woman takes her belongings and leaves my house at once? Or do you have some objection to my making those decisions?"

"No, My Lady," he replied quietly. "Whatever you say."

"Good, because if you cannot do that, you may go with her and anyone else who feels they have the right to steal from me."

He took her arm and guided her to the door but I stopped him before he left the room.

"Have the carriage brought round, please. I wish to visit my uncle."

I could hardly believe what the woman had told me. How could my uncle have deceived me like this, and what was his motive? Why did he not want the credit for his good act? Did he suppose I might be too proud and want to move into his house instead? Just as if I could be too proud for anything.

He was busy writing when I was shown into his rooms. He looked up with an irritated frown, as though I had interrupted something much more interesting and important. I realised all at once that he still treated me as the poor little wretched child who first appeared on his doorstep seven years ago and my newly discovered confidence was not going to allow it to continue.

"I was told," I began firmly, "that it is you who is responsible for my residence and for my upkeep, not the Earl of Connaught. I was told that he left me nothing, that the house was to be sold over my head. Is it true?"

He looked uncomfortable as though I had discovered a shameful secret.

"Yes, it is true," he confirmed quietly.

"Why? And why did you not tell me?"

"Why?" He repeated. "Because it was my fault, that is why. He came here, the day he left you. He was very angry and he told me he was going to sell the house and your jewels and that I had better be prepared to take you back here."

"Oh, and you did not want that did you?"

"No, but that was not the only reason. It was my fault he had left you with nothing and I did not want you to know that. I was the one who deceived the Earl into marrying you. I knew his only reason for marrying was to procure an heir and I knew that you were likely to be barren, but I went ahead with the arrangement anyway. I was not likely to find another titled gentleman to wed you, was I? I was not likely to find anyone to wed you, knowing that you could never bear a child." He paused and looked at me with a plea in his eyes. "I thought it was for the best at the time, but I was wrong. I thought he would be bound to fall in love with you, with your beauty and your modesty, and then the question of a son would be irrelevant. I did not understand how important those things are to the aristocracy."

I was shaking my head, unable to find words with which to reply. I had been very angry and now I just felt deflated. Had he really believed it was for the best?

"I loved my wife, you see," he went on. "It would not have mattered to me if the child had died, my baby son. It did matter that she died and I will never understand how a man can put his baby before his wife. I am not of the same world, Rachel. Forgive me."

What else could I do but forgive him? Perhaps he did have the best intentions, even though I begged him not to force a marriage to anyone. If he loved his wife so much, I would have thought he might have more understanding, like my new friend who was so concerned for his wife's happiness.

It was the following day that Lord Summerville returned with his Countess, a shy little thing who curtsied and kept her eyes cast down the whole time, even after we sat. This man had filled me with a lifetime's worth of confidence in a few short hours and yet I did not know which one to pity more.

CHAPTER FIVE

So I had found friendship in the most unlikely place. The Earl was so charming and so good looking, women turned their heads as he passed, their eyes followed him wherever he went. I do not believe I have ever seen that look in the eyes of a woman before, but his wife was strange, more like a child than a grown woman.

She sat and stared down at her own hands, not looking up for anything. I was the very last person to know how to engage someone in conversation, but I did my best. Every question I asked was met with a nod or a shake of the head and I looked over her head at the Earl in desperation. He merely shrugged, as though this scene was not new to him. The afternoon was dragging when His Lordship said he had an appointment.

"It will not take long, My Lady," he said. "Perhaps my wife could stay here with you." He turned to her then with a sigh, but also a gentle smile, like a kind uncle to a child. "Will that be acceptable, Rosemary?" He asked gently. "You would prefer to talk to Lady Rachel alone, would you not?"

She nodded but still did not raise her eyes, at least not until she heard her husband depart the house. Then she looked at me, and there was a discernible though silent sigh of relief. She was a lovely girl, dark auburn hair and beautiful green eyes, but she did not seem to ever smile. She was staring across the room at a porcelain doll I had rescued from my short lived childhood.

She got to her feet and walked over to the doll, then picked it up and held it against her as though it were a child. Then she came back to her seat, keeping the doll in her arms.

I asked her what sort of things she liked to do with herself and had to lean forward to hear her reply.

"I paint a little," she said. "Not very well though."

"I am sure your paintings are beautiful," I tried to assure her, but she only shook her head.

"How long have you been married?" I persevered, wondering what I would say next once that question was answered.

"Two years I think, My Lady," she said quietly.

Think? Did she not know?

"And children? Do you have children?"

Suddenly her eyes widened and she looked alarmed.

"I do not think I would like that," she said quickly. "It is not nice."

Not nice. What a very odd thing to say, and was she talking about the act that led to childbirth or the birth itself? I could well understand her reluctance for the former, though I had believed that was my own special burden.

A noise outside made her jump slightly but she relaxed again when she realised what it was. I reluctantly decided that the only way to find the answer to the Earl's question was to ask her outright.

"My Lady," I said softly, "are you afraid of your husband?"

She looked up at me briefly, then nodded.

"Why? Is he unkind to you?"

I had a vivid memory of the terrible beatings my mother had endured at the hands of my father, but although I asked the question, I could hardly believe that any woman would be afraid of Lord Summerville. He had always been kindness itself to me and I could not accept that to be merely a facade for my benefit. And if it was, what did he hope to gain from it? I would not be his mistress, that would never be my role in life, as a mistress would have needs and desires that were stolen from me.

Rosemary was shaking her head.

"No, My Lady," she said firmly. "He is anything but unkind. It is not how he treats me but what he might want from me that I fear."

"Want from you?"

This conversation was getting very personal, not subjects that should be discussed between strangers, not even two women, but I somehow felt a kinship with her fears if they were what I suspected them to be.

"Yes, My Lady," she was saying. "I know enough to know what men want from a wife and I cannot face it. I am scared that if I do not keep him away, he might try that again."

I did not want to pursue this line of conversation. I knew precisely what Rosemary meant but I did not know if he suffered from some sort of brutal perversion or if she was inhibited. I guessed the latter, as talking to this girl I felt that I was talking to a child. The wedding night must have been an unparalleled disaster if it had been two years and she still feared a repeat of it but from the looks that followed him everywhere he went, I was quite sure that His Lordship was getting satisfaction elsewhere.

It was then that the door opened and he entered. I watched his wife freeze, as though she wanted somewhere to run away and hide, but there was nowhere.

"Forgive me for keeping you waiting, My Lady," he said quietly, then held out his arm for his wife to take. She did so reluctantly. "We do not want to outstay our welcome," he went on.

They left, leaving me to ponder what had happened. I pitied this girl who seemed to have been pushed into a marriage that she could never be happy with, but more than that I pitied the Earl.

He called on me the following day, alone this time.

"My Lady," he said immediately. "I feel I ought to seek your forgiveness for yesterday. I had this idea that you might be able to learn what troubled my wife, since she refuses to tell me. It was very wrong of me to take advantage like that."

"No matter," I replied.

For the very first time in my life I felt that someone needed me, needed me for myself and my opinion and experience, not my body or my beauty. I was rather pleased, and intended to answer him, even though the subject was embarrassing to me.

"Did you?" He said. "Did you learn anything? Is there anything I can do to help her, or should I abandon the marriage as a lost cause?"

I felt uncomfortable discussing such intimate details with any man and I hardly knew him or his poor wife. But he had asked me for a favour and I owed him that much, owed him an honest observation.

"Forgive me, My Lord, but your wife is a child." I paused then, trying to think of the right words. It seemed to me that Rosemary was afraid of what I was afraid of, though I had no idea what to call it. Love had nothing to do with it as far as I was concerned. "She is terrified of the act of intimacy, if that is what you have done to her, and will never accept it as normal. That is what I learned, if it is of any use." I paused and drew a deep breath to enable me to go on. "Her parents were cruel to make her marry. I believe she is one of those unfortunate people who will always be childlike."

His expression did not change and I felt I was not telling him anything that he did not already know.

"I feel I am trespassing on your good nature, but I really do not have anyone else with whom I can share this." He paused thoughtfully, as though wondering whether to go on. At last he did and it was an intimate revelation I could have lived without knowing. "My marriage to Rosemary has never been consummated. She was so afraid I could not.." He broke off then, leaving me to wonder whether he actually wanted a reply.

"A marriage like that can be annulled, I believe, My Lord," I said quietly, wondering why he had not thought of that himself.

"Yes, I know," he said, "but it would require proof, would it not? An examination of some sort to confirm that she is still a virgin."

I nodded, suddenly terrified as I recalled that day when my mother and I had arrived at my uncle's house, when his physician had examined me after my ordeal. I was not about to recommend that be done to any other woman.

I looked up at the Earl, blushing, almost sure that he had read my thoughts and could see what I could see. And I could not believe that I was actually having this conversation with a man, especially a man I had known for such a brief time. He was shaking his head.

"I cannot subject her to anything so invasive," he said quietly. "It would be grossly unfair and it is unfair to be talking about her like this."

"What will you do?"

"I will send her back to Summerville Hall, to my mother, and promise not to go near her again. That should at least give her some peace even if I do have to forget any idea of having a son to succeed me. I was hoping that you might know of some way I could help her, or someone could help her, but if what you say is true, she cannot be helped."

His words tore at my heart, he sounded so disappointed, but I could feel his eyes on me for a few minutes before he took my hand and raised it to his lips.

"Thank you," he said softly. "And please, please forgive me. You have done me a great service this day and with your help I may be able to break away from her. We will both be happier, I think."

"My help? What does that mean exactly, My Lord?"

My mind was full of images, memories of my late husband, of the King and of my tenth birthday. My stomach heaved at the recollections.

"It means that I have become fond of you."

I tore my hand from his grasp.

"No!" I cried, shaking my head. "I will never be your mistress, My Lord, never!"

He looked even sadder all at once.

"Rachel," he said soothingly, "that was not what I had in mind. I understand, or think I do, that something was done to you, something horrendous that you would hide your beauty away as you do. How could I not notice how you flinched when I took your hand that first time, how you stiffen when anyone admires you? That is why I thought you might be able to talk to my wife. I would never ask anything of you, never."

"What then? Nobody wants me for a wife, thank God, not since I am barren. And anyway you are already married."

The concern that crossed his face at that was almost tangible, but he asked no questions. He put his arm around me and as we sat down together, he held me close to him and pressed my head against his shoulder. For the first time in my life, I felt loved and valued. It was a very intoxicating emotion.

The following day he was back again, this time with a gift.

"I want you to come for a ride with me, in the park," he said at once. "It is a lovely day and in return for helping me, I wish to get you out in the fresh air."

"No," I said immediately. "I will not be paraded around the park like some ornament on your arm or anyone else's."

"I thought you would say something like that," he replied. "That is why I brought you this."

Under his arm he had a rolled up piece of cloth and now he shook it out to reveal a hooded cloak of black velvet.

"No one will even notice you in this, and if they do they will think you are a widow and pay no attention." He stopped talking while he placed the cloak around my shoulders and lifted the hood over my hair and headdress. The cloak was voluminous, designed to cover my skirts and my entire body up to my neck. I could not help but laugh. "Most people, especially women," he went on, "would be anxious to cover themselves if they were ugly or had some sort of deformity, not because they are too beautiful."

"Most men would be wanting something from me, not befriending me and helping me to hide."

"Oh, Rachel," he said quietly, shaking his head, "do not think me immune to your attractions. A man would have to be blind not to stir at the sight of you. But you are entitled to do whatever you want and what you want is of more importance to me than what I might want. One day, I hope you might trust me enough to tell me what horrors you have suffered, but that too will be your decision."

***

So began for me a time of knowing what friendship actually was. I was distrustful of the Earl at first, wondering all the time when he would make some sort of move to change the nature of our relationship, but it never happened. While he spent time with me, either riding in his carriage or playing cards at my house, I know that he had more than one woman who was happy to give him what he needed. He did not spend all his time with me.

He had not been home to Summerville Hall in Suffolk for a year or more. He had promised his wife that he would not go near her and he had not done so, but he needed to be there in order to run his estate.

"I have had the east wing separated from the rest of the house," he told me, "so that I can be in my own house without scaring my wife. Do you not find that an amusing state of affairs, My Lady?"

He was being facetious, of course, mocking himself I think and my heart went out to him.

"I find it a very sad state of affairs, Richard," I replied. "You do not have to suffer a loveless marriage. We talked about it before."

"And you agreed with me that it was unfair," he replied quietly.

"I did, but she must understand why it is necessary. She will be relieved to have the marriage annulled, surely, and you must remarry. You must have an heir. I did not understand when it was done to me; I was but ten years old."

There, I had said it and now I wished I had held my tongue. He looked at me with a frown of curiosity, and I was very much afraid he was going to ask questions, want to know why a ten year old should be subjected to such an examination. Of course, he did not. He was far too empathic for that.

"I will consider it," he finally replied with a sigh. "To tell you the honest truth, I thought I could do this, keep my promise, but now I am not so sure. I am beginning to resent her, even wish her dead. Is that not a terrible thing to think?"

"I cannot tell you how many times I wished my late husband dead," I replied. "And my father. If wishes could kill, he would have been the first one to go."

Once more I saw the compassion in his eyes as he looked at me.

I reached out and touched his arm, and I realised that I had never before made any overtures of affection, that I had always been afraid that any sign of affection would be misconstrued. But he merely turned and studied me for a few moments and I knew that I was in no danger. I hugged him then, something that I had never done nor wanted to do before. I really, really loved this man, and I so wanted to help him for all he had done for me. He was like the brother I never had.

"I have to return to Summerville," he said. "I would like very much for you to come with me, but I feel that would be unfair to Rosemary and heaven knows what my mother would have to say about it!" He laughed then, and it was a joy to behold. "I have kept my relationship with my wife a close secret from her."

"What would she do if she knew?"

"I believe she would march into Rosemary's chamber and tell her to grow up! I think she would subject her to a long lecture about the duties of a wife and scare the life out of her." He gave a little smile, probably imagining his mother's outrage at her handsome and charming son being rejected by his own wife, when women all over London were falling over their feet to invite him to their beds. I suppose it was an amusing scenario, when one thought about it.

So he went back to Suffolk and I did not see him again for many months. I had no reason during those months to leave the house, but I had a new maidservant whose job it was to wait only on me and she was a girl who knew precisely what was going on in the city outside.

She turned up on my doorstep late one night and proceeded to curl up there to sleep. When I was told, I naturally took her in and found she was homeless and hungry. I needed a maid and more than that, with Richard gone, I needed a friend and I could feel an affinity with this girl that I could not have felt with the other servants.

She was grateful for the position and I did not believe she would try to rob me. Her name was Lucy and she was always cheerful and bubbly and if I wanted to know anything, I had only to ask. What she did not already know she would go and find out.

Queen Jane had died just twelve days after the birth of the much longed for prince and a new marriage had been arranged for King Henry. This was a foreign princess who he had never met, but he had sent his portrait painter, Hans Holbein to Flanders to capture her image. She was to come to England to marry the King without ever having set eyes on him.

My heart went out to her. I recalled my one night with the King, his disgusting breath and his wet lips, and I shuddered. This poor princess was about to commit to suffer that every single night. While I pitied her, I also hoped she would hurry and get here before he sought satisfaction elsewhere. Richard Summerville had been escorting me about London and although we had stayed away from court, I lived in fear that someone would have noticed me.

I missed Richard but I had my reading matter and my little maid who kept me company as well as serving me. Sometimes I went out in the closed carriage, wearing the black velvet cloak that Richard had given me, and watched what was going on in the park. I often passed the palace like this, but I made a special effort then not to be seen.

The King had remarried but had refused to consummate his marriage, declaring that the Princess Anne of Cleves was far too ugly. The portrait painter, had not painted a good likeness, he had made her complexion smoother, her body slimmer, and Henry had named her the Flanders Mare. I could not help but wonder what sort of arrogance a man would have to have, to be so unattractive himself yet refuse a woman on the grounds of ugliness. She had indeed had a lucky escape.

The marriage was annulled, making me wonder if Richard had thought any more of doing the same with his own marriage. I doubted that this temporary Queen would have been subjected to an intimate examination. She and the King likely only had to declare their aversion toward each other.

I hoped his disappointment with his new queen did not cause him to remember the little girl who had sobbed half the night away in his bed. I could not quite convince myself that with all the mistresses he had since had, he would not even remember me. I was too afraid of the possibility to think like that.

Richard returned just once more that year, a fleeting visit on his way to visit his mother's lawyer.

"She died three days ago," he told me despondently. "I have to see about her will, make sure everybody gets what she wanted them to have. She set aside a trust fund for her future grandchildren. How is that for a cruel joke?"

"Richard, stop, please!" I cried out. "You are only tormenting yourself. You need to annul the marriage. You know it, I know it and deep down, Rosemary knows it. Why not ask this lawyer about it while you are there? What have you got to lose?"

He looked at me sheepishly for a few moments, then squeezed my hand. I caught a little smile from Lucy as she came in with ale. She knew nothing of my personal pain and believed like everyone else that Richard and I were more than just friends."

"I will think about it," he said softly.

"You said that before, but here we are. My dear, I just hate to see you so unhappy."

He drank his ale and kissed my cheek, but he promised to ask the lawyer. The visit lasted but half an hour, yet I still missed him when he had gone.

"Lovely looking man, My Lady," Lucy commented with a little knowing smile when she came to collect the tankards.

"Yes, indeed he is, Lucy. You can admire from afar if you wish but Lord Summerville and I are friends, nothing more."

"Whatever you say, My Lady," she replied but I could tell that she did not believe me. No matter. I was quite flattered actually, though I would never have told her that.

My life continued with its quietude and I thought I could be happy living like this. I had believed that if I kept myself hidden and kept to my house and my closed carriage, all would be well.

Then my uncle died and my world changed once more.

CHAPTER SIX

The first I heard about Uncle Stephen's death was when a lawyer arrived at the house to tell me that he had left nothing but debts. His own house in Holborn would be sold and the house that I lived in, my home, would be all that was left. There would be no money for its upkeep, nor for the servants nor even for food. The house would have to be sold as I would not be able to afford to keep it.

I was desperate. How was I to tell the servants that there would be no more wages, that their home would be gone. Some of them stayed long enough to find another position, and I was able to sell some jewellery to pay Harry to make a trip to Suffolk to seek help from Richard.

I knew he was my only hope and even though I should have known better by then, I gathered my courage, wondering what he would ask for in return. Imagine my dismay when Harry returned to tell me that Lord Summerville was not at home, that he had gone to France on family business and could not be reached. I thought of making a trip myself, perhaps asking his wife for aid. She knew who I was and even if she believed me to be one of his mistresses, it would not really distress her very much. But of course, she would have no means of her own, even if she felt inclined to help, and I did not even know if he had succeeded in annulling the marriage, if she was still his wife.

The jewels that I sold were all we had and I had to budget carefully until I could find out what to do. Lucy was the only one who remained with me, bless her heart. She refused to move from my side, even though there was no money with which to pay her. I hung on for weeks, hoping that a message would find Richard, but nothing was heard except confirmation that he was in France.

He had been my last hope and now there was only one option left, and it was not one I was looking forward to.

"Lucy," I said. "I will have to appeal to the King. There is no other way."

"The King? Will he help us?"

I smiled at her use of the word 'us'. She never once varied from the united front she had set up for us.

"He might, given the right incentive," I replied with a shudder.

"My Lady, is there no other way?" She asked quietly. "Surely Lord Summerville can be reached somehow."

"I daresay, if I had the funds to send people to France to find him."

I thought then how ironic it was that this beauty that had caused me so much pain, could have saved us had it not already caused my destruction. I am quite sure that many beautiful women had happily sold themselves rather than starve but that option was not open to me.

"I will venture into the street myself, My Lady," Lucy declared firmly, "see if I can find some work to help us."

"Lucy, why would you do this for me? You can go, find work, keep your pay to yourself. I will appeal to the King; perhaps at long last this face will help me survive."

"I daresay, My Lady, but that is not what you want is it? I would have starved or frozen to death were it not for your kindness. I will go now, see what I can find. You must let me help."

But Lucy found no work, at least not enough to help us. Even if the house were sold, according to my uncle's lawyer, the money it fetched would go toward his debts. The only reason it had not been sold over my head was because of a special entail he had set up. There was no help for it; I would have to throw myself on the mercy of the King.

My message to the King's private secretary produced a response that I neither wanted nor expected, but it seemed it was the best I could hope for. I had steeled myself to offer myself to him, despite my revulsion, but it seemed that he was besotted with yet another woman. While I had appealed to the King, it had not escaped my notice that he was presently without a wife and I hoped he would not take my interest as an invitation to elevate me to that position. The reply I received was that His Majesty had a husband in mind for me.

My heart sank. Although he was no longer my servant, Harry was kind enough to make a few more enquiries for me in the hope that Lord Summerville had returned to London, or even Suffolk, but no one had heard from or seen him. I could only hope he was safe and look to my own interests. I felt sick to think about it; I knew that Richard would help me if he only knew my plight.

Damn my uncle! Why could he not have been honest with me? Had he only told me that this might happen on his death I could have been prepared, even sought help from my only friend before this. I could curse the day I had ever met Uncle Stephen, but it went back farther than that. I cursed the day I was ever born.

It was a quiet and hasty service, no preparations made at all and it seemed I was to be wed to yet another man who had no desire to meet me first. I thought I knew what to expect, a repeat of my time with Lord Connaught, another nobleman who wanted only an heir except this one was a marquis, a little higher up the ranks. But I would not be telling this one that I was barren. Whoever he was or whatever he wanted of me, I needed this marriage far more than he did.

I only wondered if there was some sleeping draught I could take so that I slept through the whole, disgusting ritual. I made a mental note to ask Lucy to try to get some poppy juice. I could give it to him, but I would rather take it myself.

I may be lucky this time, perhaps, I thought. This one might be kind, have some consideration. If I was really lucky he might even be impotent.

The church was dark and I did not look at my bridegroom. I could tell by the way he walked that he was not a young man, and from the corner of my eye I saw grey hair. But when the service was over, I turned and looked at his face and I thought my heart would stop in my chest, I thought I must be asleep and having one of my nightmares – along his cheek he bore a scar, an ugly t-shaped scar.

It seemed that God had a sense of humour after all. I had just married my tormentor, the monster who had stolen my innocence, stolen my childhood and turned me into an incomplete woman. I could not believe it!

Why did he want a wife? I was a grown woman, not a little girl which was more to his taste. I looked across the church to see if his friend were also there, but there was no sign of him.

Tears gathered in my eyes then, tears of despair. Perhaps his tastes had matured and he now wanted a full grown woman. I wondered if he had done this deliberately, if he knew who I was and this was giving him some sadistic pleasure.

I was shaking as I placed my hand on his arm and was led along the aisle and out of the church.

***

The festivities began at once with many guests congratulating the Marquis on the acquisition of such a beautiful wife and I gathered from their words that despite his advanced years, I was his first. I also gathered that I was probably the only one who knew why that was.

He said nothing to me as he shook hands and accepted good wishes and I was sure he had no idea who I was. Why would he? He must have done the same to many children, so why should I be memorable? I could not bear to look at him. Every time I tried I was reminded vividly of the horrors of my tenth birthday and I wondered just how I was going to cope with the consummation of this cruel match.

I reminded myself that I had married for one reason and one reason only – I could not survive without it. I had to do as he wanted, did I not, or I would be starving on the streets.

Lucy had come with me and now she met me in the bedchamber, ready to perform the ritual of undressing me. I must have looked awful; I was still in shock.

"My Lady?" She said with a puzzled frown. "What is wrong? You look as though you had seen a ghost."

"I have," I replied, "the ghost of my innocence. Lucy, I..." But my voice was shaking so much I could barely speak.

She did something then for which I will always be grateful. She put her arms around me and held me close as though I were a frightened child, and that is just what I felt like – a frightened child once more, indeed a terrified child just wanting her mother. But there was no mother, there was no one and I thanked God for Lucy.

The Marquis did not come. I had my sleeping draught ready, but as I suspected, he had no interest in raping a full grown woman and after an hour or more of waiting, Lucy lie down beside me intending to sleep with me.

"My Lady," she said. "It does not look as though His Lordship is coming tonight. Would you like me to stay with you?"

I nodded. I still did not feel confident enough to actually talk, my voice shook every time I tried, but I found comfort with this simple servant girl that night. I did not sleep though; I was afraid that the monster might come in the night. I could not think of him as anything else, only 'the Monster'.

In the morning he came and dismissed Lucy with a snap of his ugly, gnarled fingers.

"My Lady," he began as soon as she had gone, "I expect you are wondering why you were left alone last night."

I made no reply. He obviously had no idea that I knew why I had been left alone, he obviously had no idea who I was.

"I have managed without a wife my entire life and the only reason I have one now is that I need the help of a woman. There will be no bedchamber activity between you and I." He paused and frowned at me, looking for a reaction but I kept my face impassive. "Don't you want to know why?"

"Perhaps because I am a little older than your normal taste," I replied harshly. I did not bother with his title as I did not think he deserved any such courtesy.

He looked startled as though that was the very last thing he expected to hear. Perhaps it was.

"Have we met before?" He asked at last.

"Oh, yes, we have met before. I believe you cheated my drunken father out of his property as well as his little daughter," I replied, watching him carefully. "I believe you killed him."

He looked horrified for a moment, then he frowned as though trying to remember.

"Rachel, is it not?" He asked at last. "You see, I do remember you. You were a beautiful child, absolutely stunning. Well, well, well, fate certainly moves in mysterious ways." He smiled then, showing gaps between his blackened teeth. "It was not I who murdered your father, by the way. It was my colleague, Mr Carter. He is dead now and the house had to go to pay off debts."

"So, it seems I owe a debt of gratitude to Mr Carter then," I said sarcastically. "What do you want with me, Sir?"

"I need the help of a woman, I told you. You will see."

Then he left me to wonder what he wanted help with. I could imagine though and the idea terrified me.

When Lucy returned, and while she helped me to dress, I decided it was time I confided in someone.

"When I was a child," I began hesitantly, "just ten years old in fact, I was taken in exchange for one thousand gold pieces paid to my father."

I stopped, wondering if I would be able to go on, but Lucy said nothing. I felt her hand clasp mine though and give it a comforting squeeze.

"I was raped repeatedly that day by two men. One of them was my new husband."

"Oh, My Lady!" She cried in disbelief. "This must be the worst day of your life."

"Not quite," I replied. "But I think I know what he wants from me and I cannot do it, I really cannot."

"What do you think he wants, My Lady?"

"I know not where he is getting his supply of little girls, but I imagine he wants me to help him in that."

The conversation was interrupted by the Monster striding into the chamber and tossing a cloak at me. It was the black velvet hooded cloak that Richard had given me and I suddenly felt angry that he had soiled it with his deviant's hands.

"You can leave," he told Lucy and when she had gone he turned to me. "I have been thinking and I am quite glad that I do not need to explain anything to you. When I go to orphanages alone, the people in charge are suspicious. That is what I need you for. We will go this morning; there is one not far from here. If they believe that you want to adopt a daughter, it will make things very much easier." He paused and his eyes swept me from head to foot, then he smirked. "No one will believe that you mean any harm."

I had not yet decided what I was going to do to evade the journey, but I carefully avoided the velvet cloak and selected a red one from the chest. That cloak was chosen for me by someone who cared and I would not taint it or its memories by wearing it for this mission. I closed my eyes as I tied the ribbons at the neck, praying that Richard would come and rescue me.

In the coach on the way to the orphanage I tried to plan a way out for myself and whatever poor child he decided to take. I had to be careful. I had married for survival and nothing had changed; I could not afford to be without him. He drove the coach himself, so he obviously did not care to trust a coachman with this mission, but that could well be to my advantage.

"What do you intend to do with the child when you have had your fun?" I asked bitterly as we alighted the coach.

"She is just an orphan," he replied with a shrug. "No one will miss her. It was different with you; you were important and had to be returned. That's why Mr Carter made your father think he was taking money. I did not want to use you, it was him that was obsessed. I thought it was too dangerous."

"So you intend to kill her?"

"What else? Once soiled she will be of no further use to me."

I could not believe that anyone would talk like that and mean it. I had no weapon with me, though why I had not thought to bring one I could not say. I was desperately afraid of being alone and penniless, of being destitute, but who was more important? Me or another helpless child? I had not had anyone to rescue me, but this child would be different.

I said nothing as we entered the orphanage, as my illustrious husband introduced himself and his Marchioness and expressed a wish, a deep desire to adopt a little girl.

"Alas," he said quietly to the warden in charge, "Her Ladyship is unable to conceive. We thought a little girl would be a good choice, someone she can share her feminine skills with."

The warden suspected nothing, but took us down some stairs into a large room with many beds, on which sat many little girls, some as young as only two or three. They were each of them filthy dirty, as though nobody bothered to see to their hygiene, and all looked thin and underfed. A couple had lice running through their hair and I shivered and wanted to scratch.

"What do you think my dear?" The Monster said, turning to me. "You choose. You are to be her mother."

Me? He wanted me to choose which child would suffer the same horrors that I had suffered? It could not happen; I could not let it happen. But what could I do? If I gave him away, the warden would likely not believe me.

A man with such a beautiful wife would never need to do such a thing. That is what he would think and that is the reason he married me. Not only would it not work, but I could expect a savage beating on returning to his house; then I would be of no use to this child or any future ones.

Over the years I had dreamed of killing him and his friend, but now I hated him more than ever. If I had a knife, I would have plunged it into him with no regrets.

I reached out my hand and pointed to a blonde child of about twelve years old. I chose a blonde child so that the Monster could better see the lice running around her scalp and give me time to form another plan.

"A little old, perhaps?" He said with a frown, knowing that I had deliberately chosen an older child.

"I think not. A child of her age will be better company and more use around the house," I insisted.

He could do nothing without arousing suspicion and so I felt satisfied. I sat inside the coach with her while he drove the horses and when we arrived back at the house the first thing to do was to wash her hair and bathe her.

"Very well," he said impatiently. "Though it is hardly necessary."

While Lucy boiled water and took the child to her own chamber to bathe her, I went to the kitchens and looked about for any sort of potion that might put the Monster to sleep. I had little knowledge of herbs and the like but I knew poison when I saw it but I could find nothing so I settled at last on the poppy juice I had taken for myself. That would at least send him to sleep; given enough of it, he might even not wake up.

I mixed it with wine and took it to him. Had our positions been reversed, I would not have drunk anything prepared by me, but he was arrogant enough to believe that I would obey him as the law demanded. If the law were half as concerned with the welfare of children as it was in making sure that wives remained in their proper place, monsters like him would be put to death. I was only doing what the law should be doing. Did thou shalt not kill apply when it came to a freak of nature such as this one? I only knew one thing: I was not going to let him hurt that little girl nor any other little girl in the future, even if I had to kill him myself.

I had no qualms about the idea of murdering him. It was something I had longed to do for years after all, and here was the perfect opportunity and the perfect motive. He drank the wine and fell asleep in his chair, while I wondered what I could do to stop him from waking up.

Lucy had finished with the child and brought her to my sitting room.

"There, My Lady," she said. "Her name's Louisa, so she tells me. She seems to have little to say and she is scared stiff, but who could blame her? What now?"

"He is sleeping," I told her. "Perhaps Louisa would like something to eat. She does not look as though she has had much before this."

She took the child down to the kitchen where she served cheese and bread and the little girl fell upon it ravenously. So I had been right; she was half starved. But I had to find a way to keep the Monster asleep, preferably permanently, and I had to do it without Lucy finding out. I did not fear she would betray me, but I did not want her involved.

I need not have worried; when I returned to the Monster's bedchamber, he was dead. I knew I had not given him enough poppy juice to kill him, so it seemed that his heart had given out and the mixture was just enough to tip him over the edge. I knelt beside him and gave a silent prayer of thanks.

But what to do with his body? I could hardly bury him all by myself and I could not trust the servants. They would want to report his death to the authorities and I would be left penniless once more, as I doubted he would have made a will or even if he had, I doubted he would have included me in it. My only hope was to hide him, tell the servants and neighbours he had gone away, and carry on living there.

But I could not stop Lucy from entering the room and seeing his foul body slumped in the chair.

"My Lady?" She enquired in a low voice. "Is he dead?"

"I am very much afraid he is, Lucy," I replied without really thinking about it. "He seems to have suffered a heart attack."

"What do you want me to do?"

I smiled slightly. Trust Lucy to be thinking of how she could help me, and not how she could help herself.

"I have no idea," I replied. "I do not want to involve you."

"Well, it is late in the day for that." She said, striding forward and putting her fingers on the Monster's wrist to feel for a pulse. "What shall we do with him?"

"If we tell his servants he is dead, they will want to know why the authorities have not been informed. You and I will be homeless once more."

"I have an admirer, I think, in the form of the older man. I do not believe that any of these servants will be sorry if I tell them that he has already abandoned his new bride and gone away."

So that is what we did and while I felt guilty at involving Lucy, I could not have managed without her. She had been right about her admirer and about the servants' general contempt for their master.

I found some gold coin hidden away in a drawer and wondered if it was part of that stolen back from my father. It would be ironic if it were.

They were all happy to go and as soon as they had we dragged the body into the wine cellar, where it lie on the dusty floor to stiffen and decompose. I could not think about that; I had to decide what to do with the child we had rescued.

"She is a nice enough girl," Lucy assured me. "If you and I are going to manage to live in this place with no servants, we will need help. She is very pleased to be out of the orphanage so I think she will make a good helper."

She was right. The three of us would have to manage and I just thanked God that the house had little land to manage, no tenants and was remote, well away from the village. I am quite sure that this was the reason the Monster had chosen it in the first place, no one to interfere with his perverted pastime.

There were two horses trained to pull the carriage, but there did not appear to be any others nor saddles for riding. We spent a week or so driving the horses about the small estate, so as to learn how to drive it. It was not something any of us had ever done before.

I went into the village to get supplies and when the gold coin ran out, I found valuable jewels to sell. We brought up some wine from the cellar, so as not to have to return there again.

It was from people in the village that I learned of the death of King Henry. He had murdered another wife since I hid myself away here and married yet another and during this time had grown farther and farther away from the catholic faith. Although he still heard mass and persecuted protestants, it was said that his new Queen, Catherine Parr, was fiercely protestant and was trying to convert him. Meanwhile his son and heir was being raised by Protestant uncles and I could not help but worry about Richard Summerville who I knew was fiercely Catholic.

As to my own faith, God had done me no favours so I would not be persecuted for His sake, not ever.

CHAPTER SEVEN

I worried about other things as well, like the mouldering corpse in the wine cellar and how long we could stay here before someone found us out. The Monster must surely have someone who would come looking for him.

The three of us used only a few rooms in the house and spent most of our time in the kitchens, because it was warm while the remainder of the house was freezing in the winter. The grounds were overgrown as that was not something we could keep up and it was beginning to look from the outside as though the place were abandoned. Something else to worry me. Would someone come along thinking they could take over? I felt that I had all the burdens of the world on my shoulders, but I needed to be strong for Lucy and Louisa, especially for Louisa.

We had managed to grow a few vegetables and they were mostly what we lived on since the money was almost all gone and not one of us relished the idea of hunting animals and killing them for meat.

The morning that Louisa came running into the kitchen I thought our little world would be shattered once more.

"My Lady!" She cried in panic. "A gentleman just rode up!"

"Do you know who?" I asked her fearfully.

"No, My Lady, I have never seen him before, but he is dismounting. I came straight to tell you."

"Thank you Louisa," I said taking her hand to reassure her.

"I'll go and look," said Lucy quickly. "I may be able to get rid of him, whoever he is. Probably just someone curious about the place. I am surprised he is the first."

She went through to the front of the house where she could look through the windows without being seen, but instead of returning as I had expected or going outside quietly to persuade whoever it was to go away, I heard the door open followed by a delighted cry of "My Lord!"

When she returned she was followed by Richard Summerville, striding toward me as though he had never been gone. He took me in his arms and held me in a comforting embrace while all the tears that I had carefully held in check these past years spilled out over his doublet.

I caught an exchange of glances between my two young serving girls. Lucy's was delighted, Louisa's was puzzled, but both had smiles on their lips.

"I have searched for months for you," he told me. "It was sheer chance that brought me here."

I led him into the little sitting room where a fire was roaring while Lucy fetched ale and bread then left us together to talk.

"Where were you? I needed you so much when my uncle died; I had no one. They told me you were in France."

"I was. I had to find a place for my cousin in one of the convents. There are none left here." He put his arm around me and held me close. "I am so sorry, Rachel, that you had to marry yet again. I should have been there for you; I feel that I have let you down."

"You owe me nothing, My Lord," I replied.

"That is not how I see it but no matter. What has happened to your husband?" He turned my face up to look at him. "Why is he not taking care of you?"

What could I say? Richard was my dearest friend, indeed until Lucy and Louisa came into my life, my only friend. But could I really tell him that my husband was rotting away in my wine cellar, where I put him?

"He is not here," I answered quickly, not ready to talk about him. "Tell me about yourself, your wife? Did you persuade her to annul the marriage?"

"I did," he said with a note of regret that I did not understand, "and now I wish I had not troubled her with it. I thought I could just let her be. I was not going short of affection, after all, but I began to resent her so much. I tried to be patient, but I will never really understand. By the time I decided to confront her with it, I really hated her, and I expect that must have been clear in my tone." He stopped talking and turned to look at me. "Is that not awful? She had no help for how she was; it was not her fault." He sighed heavily before going on: "I explained it to her carefully, gently I thought. I could have got her woman companion to explain it to her, but I did not want her to know our secrets and I doubt that Rosemary did either. So I explained it myself, even though I could see she was afraid of the subject." He was quiet for a little while but I did not prompt him to continue. He would tell me in his own time. "She agreed."

"She did? That is good news," I said, but he did not seem to be happy about it.

"I promised her a house, far away from me where she could live with her companion. I promised her a pension and the upkeep of such a place. She seemed happy enough with the arrangement."

"But what happened?" I prompted at last. "I can see things did not go to plan."

"She killed herself," he said with a look of utter dismay on his handsome face. "The next day, I found her hanging over her bed."

"Suicide?" I was shocked and that surprised me. I did not think I could ever be shocked again. "But why?"

"She did it for me," he replied with a frown. "She left me a letter. You can read it if you like."

He pulled a piece of rolled up parchment from his doublet and handed it to me. I started to read out loud.

'*My Lord,*' she wrote.

"She never called me 'Richard'. In fact she never called me anything at all. The letter says more than she had ever put into words."

'*My Lord, I do not want you to blame yourself, but I can find no happiness in this world and you have been nothing but kindness itself. You deserve better. I do this for you, to release you so that you can find a real wife, one who appreciates your kindness and will be able to return your affection.*'

I squeezed his arm in a feeble attempt to comfort him. I knew that people would think him to blame and the disgrace to the Summerville name of having a suicide in the family did not bear thinking about.

"I am trusting you to keep this a secret," he suddenly went on. "The companion knows nothing. It was her day to visit her son and there was just me there. I dismissed her and put it about that my wife had gone to London to stay with my aunt and uncle. Their son was staying with me, and still is as it happens. My aunt and uncle died of plague two months ago, and when Rosemary was found nobody looked too closely." He paused and looked at me as though for guidance. "Did I do the right thing? I just could not bear to have her buried without the sanction of the church. It meant so much to her, that sort of thing."

"You mean you did not do it to avoid the disgrace," I asked, surprised.

"Lord, no! I never care about things like that. I did it for her; it was the only decent thing I ever did for her." He sighed wearily. "I tricked the priest into burying her in the family crypt, but look what she did for me. Who would have thought she had such compassion in her? Who would have thought she had the courage?"

"I think you did the right thing," I said quietly. "I cannot think of anything more right. From what little I knew of her, I think it would have taken more courage to stay alive. She was such a sad little thing."

"So, I am free now to choose another. And this time I shall choose for myself and I shall find a woman who wants me."

I had to smile, knowing his reputation.

"I do not believe it will be too difficult to find such a woman, Richard," I said with a smile.

"It will not be yet," he said. "Not until a decent interval has passed and this protestant boy on the throne has outstayed his welcome. I shall savour the freedom of not having to worry about Rosemary. Since she has been gone I have realised just what a burden she was, hovering around my mind all the time. It is such a relief not to have to think about her. I shall look for a new Countess, I shall look carefully before I decide." He turned to look at me then kissed my cheek. "I wish it could be you," he said.

I felt myself stiffen; there was no help for it, even though I knew he had meant nothing by it. That would always be my burden.

"Rachel, Rachel," he said, taking my hand. "I told you before that I would ask nothing of you and I meant it. I wish you could learn to trust me."

"I do trust you, Richard. I really do, but how much do you trust me?"

"You know things about me, intimate things, that I would never want anyone else to know. What more do you want?" His eyes met mine then and held my gaze for a few moments. "Are you going to tell me where your errant husband is?"

I knew I had to tell him. I had kept it a secret long enough, I had been afraid, and made Lucy and Louisa afraid, every time there was a noise outside. I was always frightened someone would come, someone would find him. Wives who murdered their husbands were subject to harsh punishments, death by fire in most cases. If there was anyone in the whole world I could tell, it was Richard Summerville.

"Do you remember the last time we met?" I asked him. "You told me then that you hoped I would tell you one day what was done to me. Is that still your hope?"

"Only if it is yours," he replied gravely.

I swallowed, wondering whether I would ever get the words out. I had told Lucy, had I not? I had no choice and I had no choice now, not if I wanted his help. We could not go on like this, there was barely anything left.

"When I was ten years old, on my birthday in fact," I began hesitantly, "my father took one thousand gold pieces to loan me out for the day to two men."

Richard caught his breath in shock and I looked up to see the horror in his eyes.

"I was raped that day, repeatedly," I went on. "I was damaged, inside." I had to stop, I did not think I could go on.

"Shush," he said, putting his fingers to my lips. "You do not need to tell me any more."

"Yes, I do. You have to understand if I am to ask for your help."

"I will help you, whatever it is. You do not need to subject yourself to this."

"I must finish," I insisted. "I want you to understand, not only because I need your help, but because I love you Richard, and were it not for two deviants and a drunken father, I might even have been able to love you as a woman should."

His reaction was to put his arms around me and hug me close against him and for the first time in my life, I wished I could be like other women. If only I could, if only it did not cause me pain, but even with him, the idea revolted me.

"When I was brought home there was no sign of my father and I never saw him again. I now know that he was murdered by one of the men, but I was just relieved to know that he was gone. My mother and I went to London, to my uncle the following day, but she lived only a few hours in his house. My father had beaten her so severely that she died later that night.

"The physician who examined me at my uncle's request said that I would never be a mother, but that did not stop my uncle from arranging a marriage to the Earl of Connaught.

"When I was thirteen, Uncle Stephen took me to watch the coronation parade for Queen Anne Boleyn and that is where the Earl caught sight of me. Once more, this beauty everyone envies betrayed me. He wanted an heir and I could not give him one, my uncle knew that but he imagined it would be love at first sight. He did not understand but meanwhile I had to suffer the disgusting and painful nightly ritual of a man who did not speak to me, who barely knew my name. I was fifteen when he fell from his horse and left me a widow.

"I believed that he had left me his house for my lifetime and a pension, as well as wages for the servants, but I found out later that he had left me nothing. It was my uncle who had bought the house and was paying for its upkeep, out of guilt for arranging the marriage which he knew would not bear fruit.

"When Uncle Stephen died, there was nothing left. I looked for you then, I sent a servant to Suffolk who learned that you were in France. I could not afford to send anyone to France."

"I am so sorry," he said regretfully. "If I had only known."

"You would have helped, I know. But you did not know and you were nowhere to be found and I had no choice but to throw myself on the mercy of the King."

"And he helped you?"

"He helped me to the altar with yet another stranger," I replied bitterly. "This one I did not even look at. I thought that if he too wanted an heir I was not about to tell him I was barren. I needed the marriage more than he did, as I had nothing. I would have been homeless and starving. But when I did turn and look at him, after the ceremony, I found that I had married the monster who had ruined me! One of the two who had stolen my childhood, stolen my life, and left me useless for any man!"

I was looking at my hands as they wrung themselves together. Just thinking about it was making me tremor uncontrollably, but talking about it was more than I could bear.

Finally I felt his fingers on my chin, turning my face up to look at him. His expression was one of pity, but not a contemptuous sort of pity, not the sort of pity I had seen when he looked at Rosemary.

"My dear, what on earth is there to say?" He whispered.

"Nothing," I replied, shaking my head. "There is more. Are you sure you want to hear it?"

He nodded then held me against him once more. There were tears in my eyes and a lump in my throat which made it difficult to talk.

"I was, of course, much too old for his tastes. He was having difficulty, he said, procuring little girls since so many do-gooders had started up homes for them," I told him bitterly. "He wanted a wife to visit these orphan homes and help him to trick the owners. I was to play the part of a woman anxious to adopt a little girl. That is where Louisa came from."

"You mean you..."

"Yes," I interrupted. "Even when I reminded him who I was, he still thought I would help him. He knew how desperate I was, how I had nothing and nowhere without him, but I was never that desperate. We found Louisa, crawling with lice and filthy, but managed to delay him while Lucy bathed her."

"And? What happened then?"

I sat up and looked at him, my gaze holding his. I needed to see what expression crossed his features when I told him.

"Then I killed him," I said firmly. "I poisoned him. I tumbled him down the stairs into the wine cellar and that is where he has remained."

To my total surprise, he smiled, and it was a happy smile, a smile of sheer pleasure.

"Good," he said. "Now you must come to Summerville Hall with me, you and Lucy and Louisa."

"I do not want to show my face anywhere near court ever again," I declared.

"You will not have to. I shall not be going there, not with a protestant on the throne, and if people believe you are my mistress they will leave you alone."

"I cannot let you do that."

"I was not asking your permission," he said flippantly. "Do not concern yourself. You will not be my only mistress, no one would expect it."

He kissed my forehead affectionately.

"You can revert to your own name," he was saying. "Nobody will look for you, nobody will know. Lady Rachel Stewart is about to become the favourite mistress of Lord Richard

Summerville and anyone who tries to challenge that will have me to deal with."

I watched his face for a little while, then reached up and kissed his cheek. I was so overwhelmed with gratitude, I could barely find words to thank him.

"Why would you do so much for me?" I asked at last.

"Because I love you, Rachel," he replied, while I stiffened slightly. He shook his head slowly. "Will you ever trust me? I made you a promise, remember? I promised you that I would never ask anything of you that you did not want to freely give. After the things you have told me today, that promise means even more to me than it did when I made it."

***

So we locked up the house and journeyed to Suffolk, leaving the rotted corpse of the Monster in the wine cellar. I wondered how long it would be before anyone found him, before anyone came looking, curious about the overgrown country manor lying neglected among the weeds.

The two girls, Lucy and Louisa, were very excited. They chattered away in the carriage on the way there and I noticed Richard looking at them indulgently.

"What will you find for these two when we get there?" I asked him, causing the girls to stop their chatter and look to him for an answer.

"That is up to you, my love," he replied with a smile. "They are your servants."

I shook my head.

"No. They are my friends. I do not know what I would have done without them."

"Well, then, they deserve the best, as do you. Summerville Hall is vast, there is plenty of room for you all."

When we arrived a servant escorted the two girls to bedchambers next to one another while I remained in the great hall to meet Anthony, Richard's young cousin. He was a good looking boy, about twelve years of age, and very polite.

"My Lady," he said softly, bowing over my hand and kissing it. "Richard has told me so much about you. I am so pleased to finally meet you."

We had refreshments then Richard escorted me to a bedchamber next to his own. I must have looked dismayed as he quickly reassured me.

"It is for appearances," he said. "We want the servants to think I am your lover, do we not? Servants gossip; before you know it everyone in the village will know, and no one will bother you."

I nodded then looked around at the rich furnishing and tapestries. This was more luxury than I had ever known before and I wondered why I had never realised just how wealthy Richard was.

"You will have your own house, Rachel," he was saying. "And I will arrange a pension of some kind for you. That way, if anything happens to me, you will not be left destitute again. You will not have to beg for help, you will be your own person."

"Oh, Richard! What did I do to deserve a friend like you?"

"Just be happy," he replied with a smile. "That is all I ask."

I stayed with him and Anthony for two years before my own house was built, right on the edge of the Summerville estate but about three miles from the main hall. It was a manor house of medium size, big enough for me and my servants with a small park and stables.

During the time I stayed with him he treated me as I imagine a he would treat a sister, always respectful, never forward. We ate together, talked together and often went out in the carriage. Occasionally, there would be a local ball to which he would take me, but I preferred to remain at home. I thought about the contrast that when men looked at me wherever I went, I felt sick with dread, but Richard so obviously enjoyed the same attention from women.

There were many women in his life, but he never brought them home. Instead he would spend nights away, which I would not dream of questioning.

When we moved to the new house, Lucy was my maid, Louisa had developed a talent for cooking and we had our own men servants to tend the hard work, the grounds and to drive the carriage.

This was ideal for me. Nobody would bother me while they thought I was Richard's mistress, while I was under his protection.

He had said he would not be going to court and he kept his word. He had no position there and he was not in favour with the King or the Lord Protector. They had no proof that he was catholic, but I do believe they suspected it.

There was a catholic chapel in the woods, overgrown and hidden by the trees, and I knew that he heard mass there, gaining access through the tunnels under the house. He never asked me to accompany him and I never did. I attended the church in the village, as that was the law, but neither the protestant service there, nor the Catholic one in the hidden chapel meant anything to me. I was not even certain that there was a God and if there was, He certainly had no love for me.

The years slipped by, quietly and happily. Lucy married one of the male servants and set up home in a small cottage in the village, rented from the Summerville estate. The man obviously adored her and for that I was glad;

she had supported me through everything and I was so glad to see her happy.

Although I had my own house, I still spent time at Summerville Hall. I enjoyed Richard's company and I enjoyed Anthony's. He was growing up into a fine young man and was always kindness itself to me and he worshipped Richard.

One afternoon I had called to see if either of them wanted to come riding with me the following day, when I caught sight of Richard, leaving his bedchamber with a rather lovely blonde woman. I had seen her before; she was his neighbour from the small manor house over the hill, Winterton House. So he was choosing his mistresses from closer to home now? I said nothing to him nor to Anthony, but I left, not wanting to embarrass the woman by letting her know I had seen. I knew she had a husband and exposure might be dangerous for her.

When I got home, I could see that Louisa had just returned from somewhere. Although she had said nothing to me, she had taken it upon herself to ride out to the Monster's house and see if anyone was living there, if anyone had yet found his body.

"It has burned down, My Lady," she told me when she came back. "I asked about the village and it seems it was burned down just after we left. There is nothing there now, nothing at all. They said the fire started in the wine cellar."

I turned to see Richard standing in the doorway. He had just arrived, but he had overhead and the expression he wore told me he knew a little more about the fire that had destroyed my former home.

I gave him an enquiring look, but he merely shrugged.

"Well, that was fortunate," he said with a grin. "Perhaps we forgot to put the fire out properly before we left."

"My Lord," Louisa said in acknowledgement, then curtsied and left us alone.

"It was you, was it not?"

"Not personally, no," he replied. "It seemed the best way. Perhaps the evil that he would have left about the place has burned with him."

I reached up and kissed his cheek.

"I am glad to see you. It has been more than a week."

"Forgive me," he replied. "I have been very busy."

"With your lovely neighbour," I replied with a smile. "I saw you."

"Julia? Sorry, that was inconsiderate of me."

"Not at all. It is none of my concern whom you choose to bed, but a little close to home I would have thought."

He laughed then and came to sit beside me, taking my hands.

"It has been almost five years since Rosemary died," he said softly. "I am searching for a new Countess. I thought you should know."

"Thank you. I hope you choose wisely this time. Do you have anyone in mind?"

"I do, but you will think me crass. Lady Winterton has a sister who visited her in the summer. I noticed her at once; she looks a lot like you."

I gave a cynical laugh.

"Then you had best rescue her before some lecherous deviant takes notice of her." I could have bitten out my tongue for that. "Forgive me. That was unnecessary. Does she really look like me? Lady Winterton is very fair."

"She does, though I have to say not quite as beautiful. I do not believe anybody could be as beautiful as you."

I could at last hear those words in that tone without stiffening, without feeling threatened. It had taken me all this time to accept that there was no hidden meaning behind his words.

"But I saw you this afternoon, leaving your bedchamber with her sister," I said.

"Yes," he replied, looking slightly abashed. "I said you would think me crass."

"Why? If you have designs on the lady's sister, why on earth would you take her to your bed?"

He gave me an abashed look, then smiled mischievously.

"I have never had much patience with people who say 'it just happened' but, well, it just happened."

"If you say so, My Lord," I replied sceptically.

"I need your advice. I do not want to tie myself to someone who will be unhappy with the arrangement," he began. "I thought if I put it to the lady herself, an agreement perhaps with conditions, what do you think?"

"I think that would very much depend on what sort of woman she is," I replied. "I would have killed for a civilised agreement, but most women might need a little, shall we say wooing?"

"I do not believe that is the sort of thing I am looking for," he replied doubtfully. "The last thing I want is someone running away with the idea that I am in love with her."

"Why not?"

"Because I do not believe that is possible. I have had many women in my life and I have never been in love with any of them, not even you my love. I do not want anyone to get hurt."

"Then you had best meet her, see what she is like up close if you know what I mean."

"I intend to," he answered with a little note of enthusiasm. "Sir Geoffrey holds a twelfth night ball every year. I shall make it my business to attend."

"What makes you think you will be invited?"

"I am always invited," he replied as though it were obvious. "He has to invite me, since I own half the county, but he does not expect me to attend and I never do. This year will be different." He paused and gazed at me thoughtfully for a moment. "Would you care to accompany me?"

"No!" I cried with a laugh, shaking my head. "Not if you are planning on getting to know Lady Winterton's sister."

"Do you mind?"

"Mind what, My Lord?"

"Mind my talking to you about this, mind my thinking of getting married."

"Of course not. It is not my place to mind, is it? I knew that one day it would happen, it would have to happen. And I want you to be happy, which is why I have to remind you of something." He turned to me with a puzzled frown and I went on, "the likelihood is that she will be protestant. I imagine you will want her to convert to your faith. It would be unfair to marry her without revealing that, yet what you are doing is illegal. You need to be very careful that you can trust her with the information."

He nodded thoughtfully, as though it was not something he had considered.

"I shall put it to her," he said thoughtfully. "If she agrees to convert then I shall assume that her faith is not deep. If she does not, then I shall think I had a lucky escape."

I knew he was joking, knowing full well that he kept his own beliefs a secret for fear of losing Summerville Hall, but I could not help be concerned for his safety. He would have to reveal his crime to a stranger with no knowledge of her own ideals and how far she would take them.

"I shall miss you, Richard," I said softly. "When you are married, I shall miss you terribly."

"No," he said quickly, shaking his head. "One of the conditions I shall insist on is that I keep my mistresses, or at least one of them."

I sighed deeply, feeling that I was indulging a little boy.

"And because you are so charming, I expect you will persuade her to agree," I said with an affectionate smile. "That would please me, but I doubt it will please her."

CHAPTER EIGHT

I saw no further sign of Lady Winterton at Summerville Hall and Richard, Anthony and I spent that Christmas quietly at my house. He went off to Sir Geoffrey's ball on twelfth night, leaving me to pray that it all turned out happily for him.

Even with all the hardships I had suffered in my life, I do not believe I have ever before wished that I could be someone else, but that Christmas I wished I was this lady that he had chosen to court. I could so easily have been a young girl from a wealthy family, looking for a suitable match, had my father not drunk away all our fortune and sold his little girl in desperation. I hoped she would treat him well, make him happy, even if it were not to be a love match.

I recalled the well hidden sorrow he had suffered over his first wife, how hard he tried to make her happy. This girl, this merchant's daughter, would be very lucky to get him and I just hoped she would come to know that, for both their sakes. I did not believe that he would tolerate another failed marriage. Much as I cared for him, on rare occasions I had sensed that he could be dangerous given the right circumstances.

The first time I noticed was not long after he had taken me in and spread the rumour that he was my lover. A peddler in the village accosted me as I waited outside the inn, wanting me to buy from him. I had no money with me, so I told him I could not.

Suddenly, the man's demeanour changed and leered at me like all those men in my past, a look I had not seen in a long time and it sent a shiver down my spine.

"Do not think you can look down on me, My Lady," he said angrily. "You are nothing more than a common prostitute."

I was shocked at the language, and I did not know that Richard had overheard him. He emerged from the inn and gathered the man up by his shirt.

"My Lord," the man spluttered. "I meant it in jest."

Richard flung him into the horse trough as though he were weightless. I had not realised before just how strong he was, and his jaw was clenched as he tried to control his anger.

Yes, he could be dangerous when protecting that which he loved and he loved Summerville and all it stood for. God help any woman who did not share that love with him.

It was three days before he returned to tell me of his meetings with the girl.

"She has agreed," he said happily, "to all my conditions."

"Conditions? I thought it was just the religious aspect that you were going to put to her."

"I was, but I thought I had best make my position clear and give her a chance to do the same. We needed to agree on the conception of a son, that was the most important thing."

I nodded, though I was puzzled as to why it needed to be mentioned, until I remembered his disastrous union with Rosemary.

"She was knowledgeable in that region?" I asked at last.

"Not really," he replied shaking his head, "but she knows that it is something that has to be done. Not like the last time. I had a sense that this was a real woman, not a child, and she promised me she would honour her commitment. She seems to be very self confident and is not afraid to speak her mind."

"What else did you put to her?"

"I promised to share my wealth with her if I made her my Countess and I told her that I needed her to be faithful to me, even though I would not be faithful to her."

"She agreed to that?"

I was more than a little surprised that any woman would agree to that condition.

"Yes. She wants the title, the mansion and the money. She is extremely intelligent, which I admire, and she wants those things enough to promise to convert to catholicism."

I took his hand and kissed it, feeling more than a little worried about this woman to whom he had proposed. She was very young, half his age, and she may not realise precisely what she had agreed to.

"Richard, I want your happiness more than anything. She does not sound like a good person to me, since her main objective is your title and wealth. Are you sure you are doing the right thing?"

"That is the point, Rachel. We have committed to each other and I told her what would happen if she betrayed me." He paused and glanced down at my hand, then kissed mine in return. "I think I frightened her a little."

"I am not surprised," I answered, remembering the peddler in the horse trough.

"She is her own person, though. She will take me because of who I am and what I own, and I believe she will keep her promises. She does not love me and I do not love her, so there is little danger of anyone getting hurt. I think we can develop a mutual respect, which is all either of us want."

"Then I wish you every happiness, my dear," I said softly. "She sounds hard and uncaring. Please take care not to fall for her."

He laughed a little, as though the idea of his falling for anyone was bizarre, then he held my hand again.

"Her father was practically on his knees to me," he said. "He had his heart set on a baron and along comes a willing Earl." He shifted uncomfortably for a few minutes before he went on: "I am a little afraid myself, to tell you the truth."

"What of?"

"I am afraid that I may frighten her as I did Rosemary," he replied hesitantly. "I did not do well with a virgin the last time, did I? Does that sound pathetic?"

"No," I replied softly. "It sound just as it should be. But can you really imagine Rosemary coming to this arrangement, making these demands?" I watched as he shook his head. "She was a child, Richard. She should never have been married at all. From what you have told me, this lady sounds as though she knows what she wants and is prepared to do whatever it takes to get it, even if she is a little naive."

***

I did not expect to see him until after the wedding and even then it was some weeks before he reappeared at my door. I wondered if Her Ladyship knew that he had me living so close; I wondered if she were hard headed and practical enough to accept that. But because I had not liked the sound of her character, I had been watching from a distance and I had come to the conclusion that their little agreement was not going to quite go to plan.

When I saw him, he looked happy and for that I was grateful. It could only mean that he had indeed chosen wisely and that this would be a real marriage, not the sham that his previous union had been.

"Rachel," he said, coming forward and hugging me. "I wish I could have come before, but I have been very much involved in getting to know this woman I have taken to wife."

"And are you pleased with her, My Lord?"

He smiled, a delighted smile that touched my heart.

"She is amazing," he answered and he seemed slightly mystified. "She is warm and honest and passionate, very passionate." He stopped talking for a moment and looked thoughtful and I knew he had something on his mind for which he wanted my advice, or even approval. I was right. "I want to tell her about you." He said at last.

"No," I answered, shaking my head. "She will never understand about me, not unless you also tell her my secrets. I hope you will not do that, Sir, as they are my secrets, not yours."

I know my voice took on a hard edge as I spoke, but I had been satisfied to be known as Richard's mistress, I had been happy not to feel that I was different to other women and I did not want it revealed to anyone that I was flawed.

"If that is what you truly want," he said, "then I will honour your wishes, always."

He still looked doubtful and I felt I had to try to explain. Whether he, as a man, would ever really understand I had no idea.

"Do you know what happened to me a week or so ago?" I paused while he shook his head slowly, a concerned frown on his handsome features. "I was out riding, alone, when my horse threw a shoe. I waited in the village inn while their blacksmith tended to my horse and while I was taking refreshments, a gentlemen approached me and asked if he could be of assistance."

"Did he say anything untoward?"

"Not straight away, no," I replied reassuringly. "He warned me that a woman alone would likely be cheated and he offered his services to see that did not happen, and to escort me home. That is as far as he got before the blacksmith's boy came in and told me my horse was ready and to ask should they send the account to Lord Summerville as usual."

I could not help laughing as I recalled the angry look on the stranger's face, the look of absolute outrage.

"You told him yes, of course," Richard was saying.

"I did. But that is not what the tale is about."
I smiled to recall it, then continued. "The man
was angry, I could see, but then he said:
'forgive me. I did not know you were Lord
Summerville's whore'."

A look of pure fury crossed Richard's face,
but I took his hand to reassure him.

"He meant to insult me," I told him, "but he
paid me the compliment of believing me
capable of such a role. That is why I want my
secrets kept, so that I have no need to feel that
anyone is thinking I am different."

"He is fortunate that you cannot tell me his
name," Richard said angrily.

"Your new Countess," I told him, "you do
not know her well enough to know whether she
will hold her tongue. I have spent most of my
life enduring lecherous leers from the lowest
classes to the highest; do you think I want to
know they are whispering about me now?"

"She will not tell anyone if I ask her not to."

"That is possible, but jealousy is an
unpredictable emotion."

"Jealousy? Why should she be jealous? She
agreed to everything at the beginning."

"That was before she fell in love with you,
My Lord."

I had to laugh at his puzzled frown, at the
doubtful expression.

"How could you possibly know such a thing?" He demanded. "You have never even met her."

"I do not need to meet her," I replied, feeling slightly abashed. "You must forgive me, but I have been watching from a discreet distance."

"Why? Why would you do such a thing?"

"I wanted to assure myself that you had not made another mistake. Your description of her character made me concerned that she was uncaring, selfish. When I first met you, you were so desperately unhappy." He opened his mouth to object but I raised a hand to stop him. "You hid it behind the charm and the smile, you amused yourself with all those willing partners, but that was not who you are. If it had been, you would not have been able to see so easily into my heart. Seeing you laugh like you have with your new wife has warmed my heart and stilled my fears. But take my word for it, Sir – she is in love with you."

He still looked doubtful.

"No," he said at last. "Just because she does not run away and hide when she hears me coming, does not mean that she is in love with me."

"What does she do when she hears you coming?" I persisted. "Runs to meet you would be my guess."

"Why yes, how did you..?"

I raised my eyebrows sceptically.

"I think that is proof enough," I said. "I have seen over the years since we met the way women look at you, with pure lust in their eyes. The look I saw in your wife's eyes was pure adoration, pure love. But please; carry on believing you are safe if you will, carry on believing that your cold hearted agreement will prevail." I reached up and kissed his cheek, feeling satisfied that he had chosen wisely. "Now return to your wife before she comes looking for you and finds me."

CHAPTER NINE

I was happy knowing that he was happy. Sometimes I would ride across Summerville land, for which of course I had its owner's permission, and I would see the pair of them from a distance, riding together or walking along holding hands like two children. They laughed a lot, they kissed a lot and from what I saw in those public places, in private they loved a lot.

I could not help but be pleased for him, even though I felt an unaccustomed dart of jealousy that this girl had stolen his heart. And it was clear to me that is what she had done, even if he would not admit to it, even if he could not see it himself. I saw little of him during those first months of the year, but I decided that when I did I would make no mention of it. He would have to realise for himself just how much he cared for his new Countess.

I did not want to lose his friendship, but neither did I want her to know my secrets and the very last thing I wanted was to come between them. I tried to prepare myself for a future without his company, but it was not easy.

In the meantime I had my books, my embroidery and I was learning to play an instrument, a harpsichord. I had engaged the services of a teacher from the village who was very respectful, who still believed like others that I was Richard Summerville's mistress despite his recent marriage. I made a mental note to talk to Richard about that when next we met. If his wife learned of our supposed relationship, she would be hurt. It was one thing having a mistress miles away, but one that all the village knew of was a different matter. It was disrespectful and would only cause heartache.

So I kept to myself and hoped that she did not hear about me, but I had no time to discuss it with him on the next visit I had from him. He had come to tell me that the King was dead.

"I have to go to support Mary," he told me.

He was wearing his thick, leather doublet and a sword and he looked determined. I had always known that if the Lord Protector tried to usurp Mary with his daughter-in-law, Richard would fight for Mary; I had known that all along. But seeing him here ready to do just that tore at my heart.

"There is money with the goldsmith in London," he told me, "in your own name. If I do not return, you will never have to worry about the upkeep of this house. There is enough to last you a lifetime. I never want you to be forced into anything you do not want, ever again."

"Thank you, Richard," I replied, "but please take care. I swear I shall worry and pray every day until you return. Your poor wife; what has she to say about it?"

His eyes met mine and held my gaze for a few moments, then he took my hand before he spoke again.

"You were right, you know," he said softly. "She is in love with me."

I could not help but laugh, he looked so mystified.

"She told you so?"

"No," he replied, shaking his head. "She did not have to, it was so obvious from her parting words. Rachel, I did not want her to fall in love with me. What will happen when Mary gains the throne, I do not know, but I do know she will expect me to be there, supporting her, just as my father and my grandfather before me sat at the right hand of the monarch."

"Well?" I remarked, puzzled. "Bethany will be with you, will she not?"

"That is what worries me. I have got to know her well these last weeks, and she is more honest and forthright than I had imagined. I am not sure that having her at court will be a good thing, and yet she loves me. She will be terribly hurt if I make her stay here, and I do not want that."

"Richard, I think you had best wait and see what happens before you start worrying about that. You have more important things to think about right now and you need no distractions."

I reached up and kissed his cheek, then pushed him away. "Now go, and may God go with you. Come back safe, for both the women who love you."

***

It did not take long for Mary Tudor to regain her throne. As the rightful heir it was inevitable that the people would support her and I knew that all along, but Richard's protestant wife may not have been expecting it.

I wondered how she would feel, now that there was a Catholic once more on the throne of England, something she would have no memory of. It made me feel old, realising that on the night I was 'privileged' to share the King's bed, this girl was but a baby. She had no idea about life then. She may have thought herself very grown up and practical when she had made her bargain with Lord Summerville, but she still had no clue about life in the real world. I was thankful that she had never learned to fear life as I had, that she could give her heart to a man and her only concern was that it may get broken.

She was pure and free and would never know the horrors that had been my misfortune.

I watched the torches being lit all across the country announcing the victory of Mary and I just prayed that Richard was safe. The returning tenants would impart their news to Bethany, while I would have to wait to learn his fate. Thank God for Anthony!

I came outside to meet him and he waved and smiled, so that I knew Richard was safe. I brought him inside and ordered refreshments.

"He is safe?" I asked at once.

"He is, thank the Lord," he replied. "He will not be back for some time though. I think the coronation will take all of his time, but I will keep you informed. This is a great day for all of us."

"Tell me, Anthony," I asked, "what do you think of Richard's new wife? Is she pleased at Mary's victory?"

"I have no idea," he replied. "I do not believe it is something I can know about. I am wondering why he married such a very young girl, but I suppose he knew what he wanted." He paused and looked into his goblet for a moment, as though he might find answers inside. "He seems fond of her and I believe from what I have witnessed that she is besotted with him."

"That is as it should be," I replied quietly. "I only hope this new reign will not drive them apart."

"Why should it? She promised to follow his beliefs so I am not really sure what you are saying."

"Nothing, Anthony. Really, nothing."

There was something I had wanted to say to Richard that I had not had time for before he left and I was unsure whether to put it to Anthony or not. He was very young and probably not as experienced in the ways of the world."

"What is it, Rachel? What is wrong?" He asked. "Richard did ask me to keep you safe as well as her, so if there is anything troubling you, I would like to know it."

I laughed then, wondering what Richard thought this boy could possibly do for me.

"I have been thinking that I should move away from here," I told him finally.

"What? Why?"

"Because all the village and the tenants know that I was Richard's mistress and that is hardly fair to Lady Summerville, especially if what you say is true. I saw a long time ago that she was in love with him and if she hears gossip she will be badly hurt. I do not want that."

"I think you had best ask Richard about that," he said.

"I agree, but when? If, as you say, he will not be back for some time it could be too late."

"Have you made no arrangements to see him?" Anthony looked puzzled when he asked. "I do not think his marriage will change your relationship very much, will it?"

My eyes met his for a moment, trying to see his thoughts. My relationship with Richard was not the same as the one he spoke of.

"It will, Anthony, trust me on that. He does not want to break her heart and he does want a son, that is why he married. I am hoping that when she goes to court, he will see that she can honour him and his beliefs and pay homage to the Queen."

"Of course she will. She is his wife, she is duty bound to do so."

I was glad he was so certain because I most certainly was not. I wondered briefly where this attitude had come from; probably his own father even though Anthony was young when his parents died. He certainly did not get it from his cousin.

It was pointless having this discussion with him; he did not have the experience of life to know what I was talking about.

"We will see," I said at last. "Perhaps if Lady Summerville stays in London I will be able to stay here. We shall see."

***

I decided to stay away from the village as much as possible I would ask Louisa to go if I needed anything. Lucy had a child now and although she still came to the house to clean for me, I did not want to give her any extra work. She was, however, more knowledgeable about my situation than Louisa and I had noticed a troubled look about the latter's expression over the past few months, an expression of disapproval whenever I mentioned Richard's name. I did not think she was happy about his marriage and I could not understand why. Perhaps she thought he should not have lowered himself to marry a commoner, but that somehow did not seem like her. I should have guessed it was out of loyalty to me, but I needed it spelled out.

It was in the autumn that Richard sent for his wife to join him at court for the coronation. I prayed for her a little, not something I often did, but I had this awful dread that this new Queen would drive a wedge between them and from what I had seen, she would be heartbroken.

Out in the country as we were, there was little immediate news to be had so I could only assume that the coronation had gone as planned. Bethany would be required to join the procession; she had not been raised in court circles and just the ceremonies themselves must be a trial for her. But her husband was patient and understanding; he knew there were things she would not be expected to understand.

When the wheel on the carriage started to splinter when I was out driving, I knew I would have to go to the village to get it repaired. I dared not risk driving home with it in that state, so I pulled in at the wheelwright and left the carriage with them while I went to the inn to wait.

I should have known I would get stares from people, but whereas before they were only staring out of curiosity, now I noticed hostility from some of the women and that familiar interest from the men. Nothing had changed for me, but they did not know that, did they?

Thank God the innkeeper was still respectful as he brought my ale to the table.

"Ignore them, My Lady," he said quietly. "They have nothing better to concern them."

I smiled and watched him return to his bar, but it was not long before another man came and sat at the table opposite me.

"So His Lordship has found himself a lovely new bride," he said insolently. "Where does that leave you, I wonder."

I looked at him for a few minutes, wondering whether to answer him at all. But at last I decided that to keep up the pretence would be a safer option than the alternative, a return to those lecherous stares and unwanted contact."

"It leaves me, Sir, in exactly the same position I have always been," I replied.

"Not from what I have seen," he persisted. "It is clear that she is more than a simple marriage of convenience. I think it unlikely that he will be needing your services in the future."

I wanted to throw my ale in his face, but part of me knew this was what I had wanted, to be known as the alluring other woman. It was all different now though, now that people believed

I was no longer the beautiful mistress who was making their Lord happy, but the trashy whore who was coming between him and his new bride.

"Well, Sir," I replied at last. "Perhaps we had best ask His Lordship on his return whether he needs my services and see whether he wants to explain it to you himself. It is Sir Arthur Manderville, is it not?"

He was obviously startled that I knew his name and as he stood quickly and retreated to the door, I could not help but smile in satisfaction. He did not want Richard to seek revenge when he discovered the way I had been treated, that was clear.

But the situation could not continue and I knew I would have to sell my house and move away, for all our sakes. I put it to Louisa as soon as I returned to the house.

"Move away, My Lady?" She asked quietly. "If it is what you want, I will of course come with you. I have no one else here, except Lucy of course."

"I am glad. You are a dear friend Louisa, and I do not want to lose you too."

I could feel her eyes watching me and instead of moving away, she continued to stare as though wondering whether to speak her mind or hold her tongue.

"What is it, Louisa?" I prompted at last.

"Well, My Lady, you will think me very impertinent, I know, but I cannot help it. It distresses me terribly to hear the way the local people are talking about you, as though you were coming between His Lordship and his new wife. And I cannot help but be angry with Lord Summerville for marrying that merchant's daughter instead of you." She stopped talking abruptly, wondering I am sure whether she had said too much, but when she saw I was not angry, she went on. "There," she continued. "I have said it and I am glad. I thought he loved you; he always behaved as though he did. I do not understand why you seem to feel no betrayal."

"Louisa," I said softly, "he does love me, as I love him, but not in that way."

"So because you have been his mistress you are not good enough to be is wife, is that it?"

I looked at her with a feeling of defeat. It seemed there would be one more person who would have to know my secret, one more person I would have to trust with the worst horror of my life.

"I have never been his mistress, Louisa," I replied at last. She looked startled and a little grin appeared on her lips. She obviously did not believe me. "It is true, my dear. I am not capable of being any man's wife or mistress because of what was done to me when I was a child, by that same man whose body lies burnt to a crisp in the wine cellar of the old house." I sighed heavily and caught her gaze. "When we took you from the orphanage, it was not adoption that was on his mind."

I watched her eyes widen in sudden comprehension as though I had given clarity to a puzzle she had been trying to solve for years. She did not ask questions, just came and knelt beside me, putting her arms around me.

"And that is what you saved me from?" She asked hesitantly. "I knew you had saved me from something, you and Lucy, but I never realised exactly what before."

I nodded slowly, knowing I need say no more.

"Then you and His Lordship really are only friends?" She asked at last.

"Yes. He rescued me, he saved me from being sold in marriage to men who wanted only one thing, who cared nothing for my pain, only for my beauty. Of course I love him and shall always be grateful, but now things have changed. Now the people in the village and the tenants on the estate resent me, they believe I am preventing their Lord's happiness and I know I would be preventing Her Ladyship's should she ever find out about me. I must go away, for her sake."

"But, if she understood."

"No!" I shook my head vehemently. "They are my secrets, Louisa. His Lordship has kept up the pretence for years for my sake, as has Lucy. I expect no less of you."

She nodded and squeezed my hand.

"As you wish, My Lady. We will do as you wish."

I sent a message to Anthony, requesting that he ask Richard to call on me if he should come back, but I was not expecting him. I wanted to secure his agreement before selling my house, but if he did not appear then I knew I did not need it. He would respect my wishes no matter what I did.

But a week after the coronation and late one evening, he appeared at my door.

"I got your message, Rachel," he said, kissing me affectionately. "I would have called in anyway, you know that."

"How was London?" I asked at once. I had not realised just how anxious I had been to know how Lady Summerville had survived the catholic court. "Did Bethany do well there?"

"I have brought her home," he said with a shake of his head. "If Queen Mary had not been so short sighted, and so distracted with her plans, it could have been an unparalleled disaster."

"Oh, Richard," I said, my hand on his shoulder. "Why? What happened?"

"What happened was what I feared would happen. Her dislike of the Queen was obvious, at least it was to me, and when required to kiss her hand I was afraid she might wipe her mouth afterward." He sipped his wine for a minute before he went on. "I did not think she would be safe there. Mary might not notice, but someone would, someone who understands human expressions and body language."

"Will you keep her here then?"

"She tells me she is with child, so if that is true it will be a good motive for her to stay away, at least for now."

I looked at him in silence for a moment, quite shocked at what he was implying.

"Why do you doubt her word?" I asked with a frown. "Why would she say she is with child if she is not?"

He looked guilty for a moment before he explained.

"Because when she first arrived at court, I thought it might be a good idea to try to drive a wedge between us."

"Why on earth would you do that?"

"I thought she might be in less danger of getting hurt if she was not quite so much in love with me." He sat down and looked up at me like a naughty schoolboy. "I said something about it being past time she conceived."

"Oh, Richard!"

"Yes, I know. But do you know what she did? My words were meant to hurt her, meant to make her think less of me, but she turned to me and she said: 'are you anxious to get back to your mistresses, My Lord?' And as well as my words hurting her, she managed to find words to hurt me. And I have no idea why that should be. I suppose it was her thinking that of me that hurt or perhaps it was that I could see I had distressed her."

"Richard, you have been many things to me, but I never took you for a fool," I told him angrily. "You have found something special and precious and you want to throw it away to save yourself some inconvenience. I am ashamed of you."

"I share your sentiments. I fear for her safety, so she must stay here. I just do not know what to tell the Queen. She wants my wife to serve her as a lady in waiting. I cannot allow that."

"She may forget about it until after the birth," I assured him. "It is wonderful news, My Lord."

"It is, though quite unexpected and a little too convenient."

"I do not think she would lie to you," I replied. "You love each other too much for that, no matter what foolish plan you had to drive her away."

His eyes caught mine for a few moments and he frowned.

"Love each other?"

"Yes. If you did not love her, those words of hers would not have hurt."

He stared at me as though I spoke a foreign language and I watched a light of recognition suddenly dawn in his eyes, then he gave an abashed smile.

"I have felt a certain something when I kissed her that I have never felt before, not with any of the women I have ever kissed."

I laughed a little, thinking about my one kiss with the King of England, though I could not see anything to laugh at. The memory still disgusted me.

"I cannot really comment on that, Richard" I told him. "I have only been kissed once, and it was not a pleasant experience. His mouth was wet and his breath stank."

He frowned with concern then took my hand.

"Would you like to be?" He asked suddenly. "Kissed, I mean? I am told I am rather good at it."

I could not help but laugh, but I suddenly thought I should take this opportunity, that it was not one that would present itself a second time. I trusted this man, trusted him not to try to take it further, and I cannot deny that I had wondered what his wife felt when I watched her almost melt into his arms.

I did not reply but I moved toward him, my lips reaching up to meet his. He pulled me toward him gently and this kiss was nothing like that one I had shared with the King. This man's lips knew how to give instead of take.

It was nice, comfortable, but there was no passion in me, none at all.

Then I felt him stir and I froze in horror, causing him to pull quickly away.

"Forgive me," he said at once, jumping to his feet, and he looked at me with so much compassion in his eyes I wanted to cry. "It just is not there, is it?"

"What?"

"That need, that joy. Those things were stolen from you and I would kill those men myself were they not already dead."

I got to my feet and hugged him, suddenly grateful to King Henry for sending this man to be my escort all those years ago.

"Richard," I said at once. "I need to leave this place. I want to sell the house and move far away, where nobody knows me."

He held me away from him to frown at me.

"Why? What has happened?"

"What has happened is that my role is different now. These people in the village and on the estate, they love Bethany. I am no longer the beautiful mistress making their lord happy, I am now the wicked other woman keeping him away from his wife."

"But, they cannot simply change like that. How can you say they love Bethany? They do not know her."

"For a man who is so perceptive, you can be such a fool sometimes," I told him with a laugh. "Every single person who sees you together loves her because they love you and they can all

147

see that she is making you happy. They want you to have that heir to Summerville, a son that they can love as much as they love you. They do not believe that will ever happen while I am in the background."

He shifted uncomfortably and started to argue.

"But I do not want you to go. You will be alone again, unprotected."

"I have wealth now, thanks to you. I no longer need to sell myself to anyone just to be able to eat. If I do not go, one day Lady Summerville will learn about me living so close and she will be devastated."

"Very well," he said after a few minutes. "You have the money. I will ask Anthony to see about selling this place for you and if you need more, you have only to ask. Just promise me one thing, Rachel, that you will not disappear again."

"I promise."

"I want to know that you will still call me your friend, you will still call on me if you need anything at all."

"And I want you to promise me that you will love her as she loves you. Promise me that you will be happy."

So Louisa and I moved away, closer to London, where nobody knew us, where nobody would resent me for being Lord Summerville's mistress. From the day we moved there was gossip in the new village, but I kept my black velvet cloak about me when I left the house and Louisa put it about that I was recently widowed and heartbroken. People were sympathetic and left me alone and that is how it stayed until the autumn of 1554, when Richard came to visit for the first time.

I was so pleased to see him but he no longer looked happy.

"I am sorry to bring my troubles to your door," he said at once, "but I really need your advice."

"You have a little daughter, I hear, My Lord," I said at once.

"I do," he replied finally, smiling at the image of his daughter that had appeared in his mind. "You were right as usual; I should not have doubted her."

"Are you disappointed that the child was a girl?"

He thought for a moment then shook his head decisively.

"No, I am not. I married solely for a son, I had it all arranged how things would be, but now all I care about is that my daughter is healthy and my wife is safe. And that is why I have come, why I need your advice."

"Go on," I prompted him, handing him the goblet.

Louisa was standing and smiling and she curtsied briefly.

"It is good to see you again, My Lord," she said quietly.

"And you, Louisa," he replied with a smile. "I trust you are looking after your mistress?"

She grinned then backed out of the room while I turned back to him.

"The Queen has not forgotten, it seems, that she wanted the Countess of Summerville for a lady in waiting." His eyes met mine and I shivered at the fear in them. "I have no idea what to do."

CHAPTER TEN

The idea that formed in my mind was simple enough, but where it came from I cannot imagine. Ever since I met Richard I had wanted to do something for him, something to repay him for everything he had given me, but what I was about to propose was dangerous for us both. The question was, would it be more dangerous to allow Bethany to attend Queen Mary as a lady in waiting?

"You once told me," I began thoughtfully, "that your wife resembled me."

"She does," replied, giving me a puzzled frown. "Why?"

"And you say the Queen did not really see her, that people at court did not really notice her at the coronation? That was a year ago now in any case."

"What are you getting at, Rachel?"

"I was just wondering how it would be if I took her place."

He looked at me as though he believed me insane, and perhaps he was right, but he started to shake his head slowly.

"I cannot allow you to do that," he said. "It would be far too dangerous. Supposing somebody found out?"

"There is no reason why they should and it will be dangerous for both of us; I realise that.

But what else can you do? Do you have a better suggestion?"

He made no reply, just sat sipping his wine and frowning thoughtfully. I knew he thought it a good idea from a practical point of view but I also knew he did not want to put me in danger.

"I cannot believe you would do that for me," he said at last.

"I would do anything for you, Richard," I said softly taking his hand. "You have given me a life, something I would never have had had I not met you. If I can protect both you and your wife from exposure, then I will consider it an honour."

I was concerned that Lady Summerville might find out, might learn that there was another woman living with her husband at court and impersonating her, but Richard assured me it was unlikely.

"She loves to stay at Summerville, she loves to be with Alicia," he said, "even if it does mean being away from me. I think she is afraid of the Queen and she is afraid of saying the wrong thing. And she was not raised in the same social circles as me; it is unlikely that anyone at court would recognise her. If we are careful there is no reason why anyone should find out."

So I became Queen Mary's lady in waiting, along with a few others, most of whom were totally devoted to her. These ladies agreed with every barbaric policy she chose to make, they all thought her very wise to be torturing and burning evil heretics. This was a subject much talked about within the Queen's private chambers, and each time it was she became more animated with the overpowering responsibility.

"It seems that no matter how hard I try, more heretics appear," she cried in frustration. "You would have thought they would know that God wants them to recant, for look what He has done to prove it!"

So she believed, as her father had before her, that every thought, every idea that entered her head had to come straight from God because she was the Queen.

I managed to murmur agreement, but I was more adept at hiding my distaste than Bethany would have been, as I was not one of those protestants that were being persecuted, she was. I knew every time I heard this speech, that I was doing the right thing.

Richard's protestant wife would never have been able to withstand this talk and keep quiet, much less pretend agreement. I tried to imagine how it would be for her, knowing that the evil heretics Mary was ordering to their deaths were her own family and friends.

We were all supposed to be ecstatic about Mary's marriage to Prince Philip of Spain, and the other ladies were, but my joy was merely a sham. I had never realised what a good actress I was.

When the Queen announced her intention to marry, Richard decided it was time for him to pay a visit to his wife.

"I want to go home for a few days," he told me. "I am expecting a few rebellions over this marriage and I want to see my wife, just in case something happens to me."

His words sent a chill of apprehension through me, but we set out, me for my own house, him for Suffolk. I knew she would be delighted to see him, even though he had not told her he was coming, and that pleased me.

Keeping up the pretence was hard, but no harder than having to share chambers with Richard. The servants had to see that we shared a bed and although I trusted him completely to keep to his own side, for him it was very difficult.

He slept on the trundle bed which disappeared beneath the main one during the day. He ordered that the servants were not to come into our suite until summoned, so they would not start to gossip about the handsome Lord Summerville and his beautiful wife who did not share a bed.

"I hate to see you sleeping on that thing," I told him one night when he pulled the trundle bed out in preparation for his night's sleep. "Why not come in here. It is much more comfortable and I trust you completely to stay on your own side."

He stood and looked at me and a little sparkle danced in his eyes.

"You may trust me, Rachel," he said, "but I cannot share your confidence in me. I do not think, given such close proximity, I would trust myself."

***

When a letter came from his cousin telling him that Bethany knew about me, that he had been forced to tell her, I believed that would make him return home and explain. I even had my clothes packed, ready to keep up the pretence of going to Summerville, when in reality I would be deposited at my own house in Finsbury along the way. But I was wrong.

"You have to explain now, Richard," I told him. "Do you not see that? What must she be thinking?"

"She will be thinking that I love someone else, that I am keeping that someone else at court in her place because I am in love with her."

"Precisely. You have to tell her the truth."

"No. If I do that, she will have to know the real truth. Are you prepared for that?"

My secrets, my private pain was what he spoke of.

"If that is what it takes," I replied doubtfully.

He smiled, then took my hand.

"No, you do not want that. It is better this way."

"How can it be better? How can it be better for her to be unhappy?"

"I am very much afraid that if I tell her, she will not believe me. She will be even more unhappy, thinking that I have not only betrayed her but have lied to her as well. I will think on it, decide what is the best way to handle things."

"That is of less importance than that she knows you are not risking everything for my sake. Even if she believes we are lovers, she must be made to see that you do this for her."

"As I said, I will think on it. It may be better if she thinks I am unfaithful; she will think less of me and that cannot be a bad thing."

"No? I cannot think of a worse thing." I marched toward the door, intending to leave him to make a sensible decision. "You are a fool, Richard. I have no patience with you."

***

Try as I might, I could not convince him to go home and tell his wife the truth, even if he did have to tell her my secret. I had never realised before just how determined he could be once he had made up his mind, but I could not understand why he would think it a good thing to drive away the woman he loved.

Then one day we had been driving in the park and there was a dispatch from the prison on our return, listing the names of the executed for that day. I know he hated being entrusted with these lists, that each day they got longer, but he had a pretence to keep up as well. This day he sank down into the chair with an exclamation of dismay.

"What is it?" I asked.

"Bethany's sister is on this list," he told me soberly. "She will blame me."

"Why should she blame you? Did you arrest her? Did you condemn her?"

"She ran away because of me," he said quietly. When I looked puzzled he went on. "Do you remember that day when you saw her in my house?"

"Of course," I replied, wondering where this was leading. "It was the day you told me you planned to make a proposal to her sister. I remember scolding you about it."

"Well, it seems it was not simply a casual afternoon of passion after all. I have a son, Rachel," he said quietly. "I saw him a few weeks ago when I was watching some heretics. I thought I had saved her; I sent a warning, but it seems they did not listen. I did not know before that why she had run away, but now it all makes sense." He looked so sad I wanted to reach out to him, but something told me he would not welcome it. "Yes, she will blame me."

"But Bethany does not know why she ran away, does she?"

"She does. She went to find her; that is why Anthony had to tell her about you, because she was determined to come to court and confront me with it."

That is when I got angry with him again. Why could he not see what damage he was causing?

"There is only one way to find out," I said. "Are you going home, to tell her about her sister?"

"No," he answered. "If she has not heard, let her have the comfort of not knowing."

Perhaps if he had taken the time to go and tell her in person, to comfort her as a husband should, none of what followed would ever have happened. Who knows?

"Are you not even going home to your wife at Christmas, Richard?" I pleaded. "You have not seen her or your daughter for many months. You are missing so much of her life."

"I think it would be better for Bethany if I kept my distance, just for now."

"What? Why?"

"I feel it would be better for her. She believes I have a mistress here at court, she will only resent my intrusion into her life."

"Rubbish!"

"Please, Rachel," he said softly, "let me do this my own way. The more you and I leave court on family trips, the more likelihood there is of someone finding out about us. Then where will any of us be?"

But he was unhappy, desperately unhappy with the whole situation and that tore at my heart. Now he did not even have the dalliances that he had had with Rosemary, for the whole palace believed his wife to be here at his side. He could have found company, but he made no attempt to and I thought I knew why.

It was almost a year before he wanted to make the trip.

"Can we go tomorrow, just for a day or two," he asked one evening. "I have told Mary that my wife is anxious to see her child."

"She accepted that?"

"She did. She is very jealous because she has no child herself, and now does not want to see either of us until she has got over it." He laughed at his own wit. Mary had said no such thing, but Richard knew exactly how her mind worked. "I need to go home, Rachel. I need to see my daughter, and more than that I need Bethany. If all I wanted was a warm bed and a willing partner, I need only walk a few paces. But that is not enough; only Bethany can satisfy me now."

I reached out to touch his arm and he turned and looked at me with a look of sheer dismay, as though shocked by his own emotions.

"I love her, Rachel," he said. "I wish I had met her at another time, after all this turmoil. I wish I could tell the Queen I was going home for good."

"Have you tried?"

"I have hinted, but she will not allow it. She likes to keep her loyal servants close and she has no reason to understand my need to return to Summerville. After all, my wife is here. She even asked the other day why I did not bring my child as well."

I gave him an enquiring look in reply.

"I told her I did not want Alicia exposed to the air of London," he said. "I thought it was a good answer."

So we left London together and at Finsbury we stopped at an inn, where I boarded another carriage to take me home to my own house, while he carried on to Suffolk. I could see he was looking forward very much to seeing his wife again and I was quite sure she would welcome him into her bed whether she believed him or not.

I hoped and prayed that he would make his wife understand about me without giving away my secrets, but somehow it did not seem possible. I would have to trust her with my most private memories.

I was glad of the respite away from the palace. I found it a strain beyond belief to listen to the ardent catholic talk in the Queen's chambers, to murmur agreement. The other ladies voiced their opinions, each one agreeing with Mary's of course, but I hoped I was giving the impression of the very quiet and shy Lady Summerville who merely did her duties to perfection and said little.

It was a relief to be home with Louisa. She knew what was happening, she had to, but I trusted her completely.

So I spent two blissful days in my own house, wondering if I had done the right thing by volunteering for this role at all. I thought it would make Richard happy, give him peace of mind, but instead it seemed that he was in even more turmoil than before.

I imagined him with his wife, holding her in his arms and making her understand that this charade was being performed for her sake, not mine. I smiled to think that perhaps he would feel happier on his return, yet he did not wait until the allotted day but arrived at my door late into the night. The look on his face was pure rage, a frightening look as though he could kill someone.

"Richard?" I asked carefully. "What is it? What has happened?"

He did not answer at first, just poured himself some wine and stood trembling while I waited for him to speak. I was very afraid; this man was not one I knew nor ever had.

"I have discovered," he said at last, "that my wife has been using my house and my church and my money to hide heretics and help them escape to France."

I had no idea what to say so I merely waited silently for him to continue. He was so angry I was afraid of where his words were leading.

"You remember that little cottage next to the church, the one where Father O'Neil used to live," he said at last. "That is where I found her, after I had stood half the night beneath the church altar and listened to the whole process. I have never been so angry in my entire life."

He turned and looked at me and a shiver ran down my spine. He looked devastated and full of regret, but he also looked violent, a look I had never seen in his eyes before. A vivid picture of my father appeared before me, the last time I had seen him, giving my mother the very last beating of her life. I shook my head slowly in denial - no. Richard could not have done that, no matter how angry he was. It just was not possible.

"What happened, Richard?" I asked fearfully, not really wanting to know. "What did you do?"

"How could she?" He shouted. "How could she do that to me? I shall never forgive her, never. And she will never forgive me for what I have done to her."

He sank down into a chair while I watched him, terrified of what he would tell me next, but I had to know.

"What have you done to her?"

His eyes met mine and I was thankful to see that they were calmer, but still he did not answer. He poured more wine and sat drinking it as though his life depended on it.

"She will not return to Summerville Hall," he said at last. "She will stay in the cottage, since she likes the place so much. I have told her what will happen if she leaves it. I have taken all the money and her jewels; she will be afraid to run with no means at all."

I had a vivid memory of that place. It was very old and very dark, being surrounded by trees, and it had no proper windows, just waxed screens over the openings. There was a circle of stones with a hole in the roof above it for a fire and a floor of impacted dirt.

When I had seen it first, I wondered how a priest could bear to live there and now he was telling me he had condemned his Countess to stay in it, she who had lived her life with servants and fine clothes and comfort. I knew I had to argue on her behalf, no matter what she had done.

"She cannot stay there, Richard, for heaven's sake! How is she supposed to survive?"

He looked up at me then and his eyes were cold and angry.

"I have no interest in how she survives," he said quietly. "I have arranged to leave food in the church porch. She will have to learn how to cook it."

I was totally shocked, not only by this treatment of a woman I know he loved, but at his anger, at his callousness. But he could not mean it, could he? He was just trying to frighten her.

"When do you plan to release her?" I asked after some thought.

His eyes met mine and I shivered once more.

"I do not plan to release her," he replied. "She has behaved like a peasant; I shall treat her like one. I told her at the beginning what would happen if she betrayed me."

As I watched him drinking his wine, it seemed as though I had never met this man before. He could not be the one who had rescued me, who had built me a house and given me the means to be independent. He could not be my dearest friend who I loved so much.

"I cannot believe that you can be so cruel," I protested, still not quite believing what he was telling me.

"Then perhaps you do not know me as well as you thought," he replied bitterly. He drew a deep breath in an effort to calm himself. "Rachel," he said angrily, "I had my hands around her throat! She is lucky to be alive."

I watched him carefully for any further sign that he did not yet have himself under control. I was afraid to ask my question again, but I had to know the answer no matter what it cost.

"You still have not answered my question, My Lord," I persisted. "What have you done to Bethany that is unforgivable?"

His eyes met mine and held my gaze for a few minutes before he replied, quietly, hesitantly.

"Rachel, you are the very last person in the whole world I would want to know the answer to that."

I knew then; I knew what he had done and the shock was immense. I spun around and fled from the room, wondering how I would ever face him again.

CHAPTER ELEVEN

It was two weeks before I returned to the palace and even then I was still undecided as to whether I should be there. His anger had terrified me, as had his actions, and he did not have his hands around my throat so I could only imagine how frightened his wife must have been.

Richard had gone from the house by the time I came out of my bedchamber the following morning and I never wanted to see him again, but as the days went by I started to think more rationally. Yes, Bethany had betrayed him in the worst possible way, but did she deserve that? He had gone to see her with anticipation and yearning for this one woman, nobody else would do, and he had found a colossal betrayal. How hurt must he have felt to do what he did? How devastated?

I settled myself into our apartments at the palace and waited for his return in the evening. I had no real idea if he was in the building at all; I half hoped he had returned to Summerville Hall to release his treacherous wife from her prison in the woods. A love as deep as theirs could not end like this.

I felt sick with fear when I heard him coming and that feeling distressed me more than anything. I had learned to trust him, he was the only man in the world I did trust and now that trust had been shattered.

I felt myself go rigid as he opened the door, but he stood still when he saw me.

"You came back," he said. "Thank you."

He walked toward me and I cringed away. I hated myself for that but I had no help for it. He raised his hands in a gesture of surrender and stopped some distance away.

"You are perfectly safe, Rachel," he assured me. "My depravity does not extend to forgetting my responsibility to you."

He looked defeated, as though there was nothing more that life could do to him. I wanted to comfort him, to hold him in my arms, but I was afraid.

"I have no idea how I am ever going to make this up to her," he said at last as he poured himself some wine, then held the flagon up to offer it to me. I shook my head.

"You could start by letting her back into Summerville Hall," I answered.

"No," he replied in as tone that would bear no argument. "She is better off where she is."

"So you are still angry with her?"

"I am unsure how I feel about her now. I trapped her in the cottage to frighten her, yes, to punish her, but while she is afraid to leave it, she is safe. Do you understand?"

"I think so, but still it seems a little harsh. She is your wife, Richard, and you do love her."

"Do I?" He still looked defeated. "I am so ashamed, I have no idea what I feel apart from that. I used my strength to intimidate her; that is despicable. What has she turned me into? Or has this always been me, lurking beneath the charm?" He stopped talking and took a long drink from his goblet, then he looked at me with such distress in his dark eyes, I could have cried. "I raped her, Rachel!" He said. "How are you even speaking to me?"

Somehow just knowing that he was so ashamed made his actions seem so much more forgivable. And that hateful word just did not seem to apply. I sighed deeply, letting out some of the tension that was making me stiff and uncomfortable.

"She is a grown woman," I said at last, "and your wife. She will get over it."

His eyes met mine and I was saddened by the look of despair in them.

"Even Rosemary never made me this angry."

"That is because you did not love Rosemary," I told him.

"If this is what love does, then I was happier without it." He turned away from me and went to pour wine for us both. "Are you staying?" He asked, passing me the goblet.

"I will if you need me to," I replied.

"I would not blame you if you decided to go, to never see me again."

"Richard, I can only imagine how you feel right now, but you are a good man and Bethany knows that. She will forgive you."

"I cannot think of it now. Anthony's sister is coming from France in the next few weeks, a last visit before she takes the veil. She is fiercely pious, perhaps even more so than the Queen herself. Bethany will definitely be safer where she is." He paused and looked at me for a moment. "Besides, while she is trapped in the cottage, she will have no further opportunity to betray me."

He seemed to have calmed down a little, so I thought it might be my only chance to voice what I had been thinking.

"Richard, you married an independent woman then you let her believe that the man she loved, the man she worshipped, was risking his life to keep another woman close." I paused and watched his expression for signs of anger, but there was only interest in what I was saying. "What did you think she would do? Sit and wait for you to favour her with some attention?"

"So you are saying it was my fault?"

"Partly, yes, I think it was. I did ask you a long time ago to explain about me. I suppose you have not done that, even now?"

"There was no point," he answered despondently. "It is too late for that now."

"Why do you say that?"

"I would have thought it was obvious. She betrayed me, Rachel. She no longer loves me; I have destroyed that, it is gone."

"I doubt that very much, my dear," I told him and at last felt comfortable in putting my arm around him. "She still loves you and always will, no matter what you do. And that makes her courage all the more admirable."

"You admire her? You approve of what she has done?"

"I approve of the courage it took, yes. Do you believe that she risked so much just to avenge herself on you? Or do you think she did it to help her friends?"

He made no reply, so I waited, wondering whether he intended to reply at all.

"I am not sure," he said at last.

"Well, I am. I doubt she even thought about betraying you, much less getting revenge. She likely found out that her sister had died helping her cause and she felt she needed to do the same." He turned to face me and I was glad I had got his attention. "You were not there. You were in London, with another woman, one you loved enough to risk a charge of treason for. That is how she saw it because you thought it best not to tell her the truth. The blame is not all hers, Richard. Trust me on that."

***

That was our last year at court, of keeping up the charade of being man and wife, and the last year of Mary's reign. She had been looking ill for a long time and things went wrong, one after another. First two imaginary pregnancies and the loss of the Spanish prince, then the loss of Calais. She became less and less rational and began to see conspiracies everywhere she looked, and she looked most at her ladies in waiting.

"You have never told me your own thoughts on the heretics, Lady Summerville," she said to me one day.

"No, Your Majesty," I replied nervously. "But I agree with you, of course."

"Do you? Does anyone really agree with me, or do they say that to keep me appeased?"

"I am sure I cannot speak for others, Your Majesty," I replied.

This talk was making me nervous and I longed to be out of her presence. Then she said something that turned my blood cold.

"Your husband is not as attentive as he once was, My Lady," she said coldly. "Does he too agree with me?"

"I could not say what he thinks, Your Majesty."

"Could you not? You *are* his wife are you not?"

There was something in the way she said it, in the emphasis of the words, that made me wonder if she had discovered something of the truth of our relationship. My heart started to thunder in my chest and I was grateful when one of the other ladies entered and began to talk of other things.

I met Richard in the gallery, anxious to tell him my concerns, but his expression stopped me.

"Alicia is ill," he said. "I need to return to Summerville today."

"I will get my things packed at once," I told him, then ran to our chambers to supervise. But I took more than enough for a stay, I took everything I owned. I was afraid and I had no intention of coming back.

We had no opportunity to talk until the carriage had moved away and even then I had to speak quietly, so that the coachman would not hear.

"The Queen is becoming suspicious," I told him.

He turned to me with eyes that were dull with sorrow. I had not realised when he said his little girl was ill, just how ill she was.

"Richard? What is it?"

"She has the smallpox. I have only just got this despatch, it went to Richmond first. She will likely not recover."

And he had missed so much time with her. This year had been a burden to him I know, after the terrible argument with his wife and now this. He needed to be home, he should have gone weeks ago.

He dropped me at the inn near my house as always, but he gripped my hand as I was about to step down.

"Leave here," he whispered. "The house in Suffolk is still empty, you can move back in there for now. If what you say is true, it is no longer safe for you here."

I had not thought he had heard me, but obviously he was paying more attention than I thought. Perhaps he, too, had noticed a change in the Queen's affections.

So Louisa and I prepared to return to Suffolk, while Richard went home to his child and, I hoped, his wife.

I wondered how that lady had fared, tending to her own needs and hiding away all this time, but I thought it likely that someone who had the courage to do what she had done would soon manage to cope with anything. Unlike myself, who, when faced with the possibility of having nothing, had thought of no other way out except hateful marriage to hateful men. She certainly had more courage than I.

CHAPTER TWELVE

Anthony was the first to come and visit me at the old house. I could see from his expression that he was distressed and my heart sank. Despite the vicious disease from which the little girl suffered, I had hoped and prayed she might recover.

"Alicia?" I asked at once.

He nodded.

"She died this afternoon. Richard is devastated."

"Of course he is," I replied. "And Bethany?"

He scowled at me as though I had used a dirty word.

"He has allowed her back in the house, despite her betrayal. He has sent my sister back to France so that she will not suspect that Lady Summerville is a heretic."

"I meant how is she coping with the loss of her child?"

He shrugged, as though it were of no importance, and I was shocked.

"You have changed, Anthony," I told him. "You were always fond of her."

"That was before. I have no idea why he has forgiven her, after the way she behaved he should have put her away for good."

"I am sure she had her reasons," I said quietly, a little uncomfortable about the turn this conversation was taking. "And I am sure he had his." I found myself wanting him to leave.

"The funeral will be in the morning," he was saying. "Then Richard's wife will return to live at the Hall as though nothing has happened. What do you think of that, My Lady?"

"I think that is how it should be," I told him firmly. "I am quite sure Richard knows what he is doing."

He sighed heavily.

"So now you are back will you be taking up your rightful position? I must say I am very pleased to see you."

I had never met the child that was lost, but I had wanted to grieve on her parents' behalf. Anthony was making me angry and I could scarcely believe what he was saying. He had always been fond of Bethany and now he thought his cousin was going to take up with his mistress where he supposed he left off, while his wife mourned her loss alone. I could not bear it.

"Richard loves his wife, Anthony," I said, "and if you love him, you will support whatever decision he makes with regard to her. And those decisions will not include me."

"What are you saying?" He demanded angrily. "That now she is back he will just abandon you, after everything you have done for him and for her? I do not believe he would do that."

"Of course not. But the decision is mine. He does not want Bethany to find out about me, to find out that I am living so close. You must honour that, Anthony, or he will be furious."

"I will honour it, but I think it would do her good to know."

"It is not your decision to make. You must go now. Richard needs you at the funeral, and if he wants you to look after his wife while he is at court, then that is what you must do."

He got to his feet and took my hands in his in a comforting gesture.

"If only you could have given him a child, he would surely have married you."

That made me even angrier, that he assumed I was just heartsick and wishing I was in Bethany's place. How dare he?

"What makes you so sure I would want to marry him?" I replied harshly. "You do not know everything, Anthony, so please do not presume to make wishes on my behalf."

When he had gone I sat before the fire and thought about the whole situation, all the misunderstandings and I worried about Richard. I knew that the Queen had suspicions now and I was terrified of what she would do. As always he had made sure that I was safe, back in Suffolk and with my real name, but what of him?

I was glad to be back though, to see Lucy and her children although I had learned that I did not really like children very much. Perhaps it was a barrier I had built around myself to assuage the disappointment of never being able to have any.

Louisa was still with me and still no sign of a man in her life.

"After what men have done to you, My Lady," she told me when I asked, "I do not think I would want to trust one of them."

"Louisa, I hope my own fears have not spoilt your life. Not all men are wicked; look at Lucy's husband. Look at Lord Summerville.

She gave me a sideways look as though she knew more than she was letting on.

"Even he is not perfect, My Lady," she said. "I think I will stay as I am, if that is satisfactory to you."

She could do that, could she not? If I were to die tomorrow, she could go and find work as a servant anywhere. She could do laundry, cooking, anything to earn her keep, while I ran into the arms of the next monster I could find. Were the horrors of my life something I could have avoided after all?

I kept away from the village. I recalled the gossip about me before, and I was quite sure that while they all welcomed Lady Summerville back amongst them, nobody welcomed her husband's mistress. I could not stay here for long, that was clear, but for now I needed the respite I attained by simply living quietly and riding out to watch what was going on.

Anthony visited, but not as often as before and for that I was thankful. He said that he was obliged to keep a close watch on his cousin's wife, for fear she would betray him again. He did not trust her and never would.

That saddened me, as I could see an even wider rift being built between Richard and Bethany if Anthony had anything to do with it.

***

The year was moving on and still no word from Richard. I had been worried enough when he went back to court; now with no word I was getting quite frantic and was on the point of sending a messenger to find out what was happening with him. I was quite sure that Mary had discovered our deception and I feared what that would mean for him.

It was late one November afternoon that Anthony strode into my sitting room with a look of sorrow on his face. I jumped to my feet.

"Anthony?" I asked, stepping toward him. "What is it? What has happened?"

He handed me a letter, still sealed with Richard's seal.

"He managed to sneak it past his wife," he said. "Actually gave it to her, rolled up in a letter to me." He stopped abruptly then sank down into a chair while I poured him wine. "He has been condemned for treason, Rachel. The Queen has discovered the deception."

I sank back down, my legs giving way beneath me, and I just stared at him. I felt paralysed, numb with shock and guilt. It was all my idea, was it not? I was to blame then. It would not have happened were it not for me. And he made quite sure that I escaped, even in the midst of the worst grief of his life he still made sure that I escaped.

"You had better read it," Anthony was saying, indicating the letter which was still sealed, in my hands. "I have no idea what it says, but it must be important or he would not have taken the risk."

I looked down at the parchment as though it were something strange and unfamiliar that I had never seen before. What I wanted to do was scream, but instead I started to shake.

I tore the seal open at last, trembling so much I could barely see the words.

"My dearest Rachel," it read, *"I have always kept your secret as I know how much that means to you, but if you could find it in your heart to reveal it to my wife, I shall die happier. I tried to tell her that it was all done to keep her safe, but I am not sure she believed me and even if she did, she still believes that you and I have been lovers. I will rest much easier in my grave if she knows that I have always been*

faithful to her. Consider it a dying man's last request and know how much your friendship has meant to me. Be safe, my dear, be happy. Goodbye. Richard."

Tears flooded down my cheeks and I tried hard to swallow the awful ache in my throat. What would I do without him?

"This is all her fault!" Anthony cried out suddenly. "If she had followed his wishes as a wife should, he would still be free and you would not have had to risk so much either. I shall never forgive her."

"No Anthony," I said, reaching out to touch him. "Bethany will suffer enough because of this; she needs you on her side."

"Why do you defend her?"

"Because I admire her courage and I know how much Richard loves her." I looked down once more at the familiar handwriting on the parchment. "How did you get this?"

"I told you. He slipped it inside a letter to me with his will, then he asked Bethany to bring it to me."

"So she has seen him?" I asked, my admiration growing. "She has been to that awful place?"

"She insisted on going, despite him sending word that she was not to attempt it."

"Because he did not want her to risk her own safety, but she went anyway. Despite believing that he loved me, not her, she still made the journey just to see him one last time. Can you not see why I admire her?"

He still looked unconvinced and I was in no mood to argue further with him.

"We will lose Summerville," he was saying. "We will lose everything."

"Where will you go?"

"I have a house my father left me."

"And Bethany? Where will she go?"

It would be the greatest irony if after everything Lord Summerville had given me, the only place left for his wife was with me, in a house that he paid for. If that was to be the case then I would have to convince her of the truth.

I had an awful vision of her being in my own position, having to marry someone she despised to keep from starving. But then I recalled that she had lived as a peasant for almost a year, she had lit fires and cooked food and kept warm, all alone. She would survive; she was not weak like me.

"I will invite her to live with me," Anthony was saying, "but only for the sake of Richard's memory. Hopefully she will find another husband before long and leave."

I shook my head, wondering how one man can be so perceptive, yet his cousin had no idea.

"If you are inviting her to your house," I said, "you had best be prepared to make it permanent. She will never marry another man."

He made no reply, only looked at me as though he was not sure whether to believe me or not.

"I shall go and see her tomorrow," I said, though it was not a task I relished. "I shall wait till after the...till after. Richard wants me to tell her something, something important and dear to his heart."

"She will recognise you, so if you are planning to pretend there was never anything between you, it will not work."

"Recognise me? She has never seen me."

He was nodding.

"She has. She went to London, despite my pleas. She waited and followed you both to the park. That is how she came to be there when her sister died."

I caught my breath at that. I had no idea that she had witnessed the horrific death of her own sister; no wonder she felt compelled to help the cause. Surely even Richard must see that.

"Would you leave now, please," I asked him. "I wish to mourn alone."

He nodded then stood and squeezed my hand before he made his way toward the door.

"You know where I am if you need me," he said reassuringly.

It should be Bethany he was telling that to, not me, but it was pointless trying to convince him of that. He was going to blame someone, and she seemed the proper person to him.

Perhaps as time went on he would realise how wrong he was.

I cried myself to sleep that night, and I was sure that Bethany would be doing the same. In the morning I staggered down the stairs at dawn to watch Louisa lighting the fire. I had never really noticed before how that was done and I doubted that Bethany had either when her husband imprisoned her in a peasant's cottage. I wondered if she had ever taken the trouble to watch it done, as I was doing now.

Richard had assured me that this house and the Finsbury one were both in my own name, that no one could take them away from me, but still I worried.

I had to tell Louisa and Lucy what had happened. They both thought highly of Richard; they would both be devastated. But I waited until the afternoon, thinking that I would give Bethany time to grieve a little before I appeared and rocked her world even more. I would lose the element of surprise if she knew who I was, if she recognised me as soon as I arrived at the house. It may even mean she would not listen to what I had to say, but it was Richard's last request; it was of vital importance that I made her believe me.

I had my horse saddled and rode toward the village. I had avoided the place since I had been back, but I wanted to go there today to visit the church and the priest within it. I did not willingly attend mass, but I felt it would please Richard if I at least lit a candle of him.

I drew rein when I saw Bethany enter the porch. I had not expected to see her there as I knew perfectly well she paid only lip service to the Catholic faith. Perhaps she, too, wanted to light a candle and say a prayer and had nowhere else to go.

I turned back and waited at a safe distance till I saw her ride back toward Summerville Hall. I went into the inn then, half expecting to be refused service, but I was given some ale and left in peace for a little while. I could see that everyone knew what had happened and I could see that they were all grieving. Even though no one spoke to me, I felt that I was one of them in my grief.

"It is all right, My Lady," the innkeeper remarked. "We all loved him, and I think you did too. You are as entitled to your grief as any of us, if not more so."

I thanked him and drained the tankard, then I summoned enough courage to ride to see Lady Summerville.

I rode slowly, not only because it was damp and misty, but because I had no real desire to get there at all. I hated confrontation and I was going to meet a woman who believed I had been giving to her husband that which only a wife should give.

How would I ever convince her that was not the case, that never could be the case? Especially if she saw in my eyes how much I loved him, how much I grieved for him.

But as I approached the house the sight that met my eyes first made me believe I was still in bed and dreaming, but then when I realised I was awake, made my heart dance with joy. Through the windows at the front of the house, I saw Richard, holding his wife in his arms once more. He looked up and saw me and smiled then he mouthed a 'thank you'.

He was not a ghost, he was real flesh and blood and I wanted to jump off my horse and run inside to fling myself at him.

But that privilege was hers, not mine. I turned my horse around and rode back to my own house.

It was later that day that Louisa came running in with the news she had just heard in the village.

"The Queen is dead, My Lady," she said excitedly. "That is why His Lordship escaped. We have a new Queen now, Elizabeth, and she has spared all her sister's enemies."

"Elizabeth," I sighed. "Another protestant on the throne."

"Yes, My Lady," Louisa said with a smile.

I had never really wondered about the religious leanings of Lucy or her. I did not care either way so I assumed they felt the same. But

I knew what Mary's death meant to me. It meant no more burnings, it meant I was no longer in danger of being found and charged with treason, it meant Lord Summerville once again where he belonged, with his wife, making more babies.

It meant that I would have to leave. I could perhaps return to the Finsbury house now that I was not in any danger, but I would try to talk to Richard about it when I got the chance.

I had the chance sooner than I thought I would, for he arrived at my door that evening, with his wife at his side.

CHAPTER THIRTEEN

Bethany's Journal

I woke that morning thinking I had nothing, believing myself a widowed pauper, only to have Richard back with me, where he belonged, and telling me he loved me, yes *me*, not the beautiful Rachel, but me. He said there was nothing between them, but I could not really believe that. She was so beautiful, so exquisite and he was so handsome, so seductive. No, I could never believe that.

But I had to put her out of my mind; I had to thank her for the risk she took and pray she was able to move on with her life without Richard in it. I may learn later that I would have to share him with her, but even that did not seem to matter too much that day. If she loved him even half as much as I did, it would break her heart to give him up.

I did not want him to know how Anthony had spoken to me. It seemed petty somehow to spoil his homecoming with complaints. I knew why Anthony resented me so much and I could understand it a little now I knew why my husband had presented another woman to the Queen as his wife. Anthony was right - if I could have only followed his wishes and beliefs, as I promised to do, he would have stayed safe.

He would never have been imprisoned in the Tower, never have faced the prospect of the executioner's axe. Instead, I had driven him into the arms of another woman.

"Richard," I heard Anthony's incredulous voice from the doorway and sat up from where I had been pressed against Richard's chest. "Richard!" He repeated, coming forward and shaking his hand. Then as Richard got to his feet to greet him, he took him in a hug of sheer joy.

"Mary is dead," I told him. "Richard is home with us."

I emphasised the us, by way of an olive branch, but he did not look grateful. In fact, he scowled at me as though I had no right to be there. Perhaps he would never forgive me, but I could do nothing about it and I was far more concerned that Richard should forgive me than him.

But as I suspected, Anthony's expression was not lost on Richard. He noticed at once the tension in the air.

He took my hand to pull me up, then started to move toward the door.

"I will talk to you later," he told Anthony quietly. "For now, I need to be alone with my wife."

Those words sent a thrill of anticipation throbbing through me. It had been so long, not since Alicia was a baby and he had come home to try for a son. Or had he? It is what I believed then, but now he was telling me of feelings of which I had never suspected him.

Holding my hand in the warmth of his own, he led me to our bedchamber while I felt Anthony's hostile gaze following me. He undressed me, just as he had in the first days of our marriage, kissing my lips, my neck, my breasts, lifting me on to the bed and loving me once more.

As I lie in his arms, feeling his bare flesh against mine, his hardened nipples pressing into my own, I knew that whatever had gone before, it was over now. The pain, the heartache, the helpless longing for him and the hatred I had tried hard to hold on to, all over. I wanted to stay there forever, just lying in his arms.

"What is the matter with Anthony?" He asked at last.

"Nothing," I replied. "He is not happy with me, but he will get over it I am sure."

"He had better."

"You must not blame him, Richard," I said, looking up into his eyes. "He adores you and he believes I was to blame for putting your life at risk. He is right and I shall never forgive myself."

"No, he is not right. I will have my wife treated with respect in her own house, or there will not be space for both of you."

I pressed my face against his chest and kissed it.

"I do not wish to be the cause of an argument between you," I protested. "Let it go, please."

"We shall see," he replied then gave a deep sigh before he went on. "Bethany, I have a confession."

I wanted to find some clue in his expression, but I was afraid to look. I just held on tighter in case he tried to slip away.

"Confession?" I asked hesitantly.

"Yes," he said. "About Rachel."

Oh, God! So he does love that woman after all!

"I want us to have an honest, fresh start, no secrets, nothing to come between us. I said there was nothing between Rachel and I but I can see you do not believe me. I need you to believe or she will always stand between us. I want to tell you about her and I need you to believe me, because I will be breaking a sacred vow by telling anyone without her permission."

I sat up and looked down at him then, very much afraid of his next words. He smiled at me, reached up and touched my face gently.

"What you have to believe, first and foremost," he said, "is that I love you and I have always been faithful to you, since the day we first met."

I smiled. How did he expect me to believe that?

"You have lived with a very beautiful woman all this time, one who was your mistress before I came along according to Anthony. Do you really think I will believe you were not tempted?"

"I did not say I was not tempted," he replied with a mischievous smile. "I said it did not happen; it has never happened. Rachel and I have never been lovers, not in all the years I have known her."

"But Anthony told me she lived here with you," I said.

"She did, but not as my mistress although that is what he was meant to believe. That was a rumour we started to protect her. Her story is a tragic one, and I know she wants no one to know it. That is why it is so important that you believe what I tell you and keep her secret. She is different, and she is afraid of people gossiping about her." He paused then pulled me down to lie beside him. "Do you want to hear it?"

I nodded. Of course I wanted to hear it. If he could tell me anything to convince me that their relationship had been purely platonic, then of course I wanted to hear it.

So he told me about her, about her childhood horror, about her two marriages, about the protection he had given her and how the deception which protected me was her idea. When he had finished, there were tears running down my face and all I could see in my mind's eye was that poor little girl, the horror she must have suffered and at the hands of her own father as well. I had believed my father uncaring for wanting to marry both me and my sister off to anyone for a title, but he would never have done anything like that.

Then he told me that she did not live in London but here, next door to Summerville land, that she moved away because she had not wanted me to hear the gossip and believe he kept his mistress close by. She gave up his protection out of respect for me.

"Do you believe me?" He asked at last.

"I hope you could not have made that up?" I replied.

I reached up and kissed him tenderly, but my mind was in a whirl of memories, good and bad. This man was an enigma, a puzzle.

I had made him angry enough to imprison me to fend for myself in that freezing cottage, yet he could do all this for Rachel to protect her. I felt that familiar stab of jealousy once more but I recalled his reasons for keeping me as he did. It seems she got the more comfortable part of the bargain, but what I got I deserved; she did not.

"She was very angry with me for what I did to you," he went on. "I did not think she would ever speak to me again."

"I have tried to understand why you did what you did," I assured him. "But it is hard. I know I betrayed you, and I know I likely deserved what I got, but feeling the hatred coming from you broke my heart. I am not sure

I will ever forget that, and I would not blame you if you never forgave me. I made you lose your temper. Do you remember telling me you had an uncontrollable temper?"

"I do."

"You told me a lot of things that day that I chose to ignore. I betrayed you and I do not blame you for being so angry with me. I did at the time; I was terrified."

"Rachel told me the reason I was so enraged was because I loved you, that no one else could have made me that angry."

"Was she right?"

"She was," he replied then he kissed me again and we made love once more before we dressed and reappeared downstairs.

Anthony looked up as we approached and I squeezed Richard's hand.

"Let it go," I whispered. "Please."

"Bethany could you leave us, please," he replied.

My eyes met his and held his gaze for a few moments, silently pleading with him to do as I asked, but I could see his decision was made, so I left them alone but not out of earshot. I wanted to be sure to hear what was said.

"Richard," Anthony began at once, shaking his hand once more. "I am so relieved to see you. We thought you were dead, we thought we had lost you."

"Who is 'we'?" Richard asked him.

"Why me, Rachel........"

"And Bethany?"

"Yes, of course and Bethany," Anthony finally looked concerned at the turn the conversation was taking. "She was devastated, Richard. She even went to the church to buy masses for the dead."

Richard raised his eyebrows and I could tell my actions had pleased him.

"Did she indeed?" He asked coldly. "Then you are in agreement with me that we put the past behind us?"

"I am not sure what you mean," Anthony protested. "What lies has she told you?"

Had he not said that, had he not accused me of lying, our entire futures might have been different. He might have stayed, resumed his place in Richard's affections, but his accusation took him too far in Richard's eyes. I could see things would never be the same.

Richard's face darkened in fury and I wanted to run and get between them, before he decided to strike his young cousin. I did not want this.

"Oh, I think you know perfectly well what I mean, Anthony," Richard replied in a cold voice. "I saw the way you looked at her. Far from reporting your attitude, she wants me to let it go, but that is up to you. I will have my wife treated with respect. Do you understand?"

"She betrayed you," Anthony argued. "She almost cost you your life."

"She had her reasons," Richard answered. "She was not solely to blame. Do you understand?"

Anthony nodded but he did not look happy.

"Will you go to see Rachel. She will be grieving as well," Anthony asked. "Or shall I tell her?"

"She knows already," Richard replied. "I saw her earlier from the window and she saw me. I imagine she had ridden here to comply with my wishes, as you should be doing, but seeing me alive and well, she thought there was no longer any need."

Rachel came here, while I was still reeling from having him back in my arms? I could easily guess what wishes he had asked her to convey to me. He wanted her to tell me her secret and that is why she had come. Her secret that she never, ever wanted anyone to know, she was willing to tell to me because he asked her to, because his last wish was for me to believe he had been faithful. Would I have believed her? I could not say, but had she told me the same story Richard had, I would have had to.

I felt a swell of gratitude for this beautiful woman who had haunted my dreams for so long. I could no longer hate her, that was for certain.

I stepped into the great hall then to interrupt the tension between the two cousins, but I could see they were both still very angry.

Anthony gave me a scathing glare, and Richard took a threatening step toward him.

"Please," I cried out. "Please do not argue about me."

"I have no wish to," Anthony replied. "But I would like to understand why my cousin should forgive such a betrayal as yours."

"You have no need to understand," Richard told him. "The decision is mine alone."

Anthony was shaking his head and still looking at me with loathing, as though he thought I had somehow forced his cousin into taking me back. What on earth did he think I could possibly do to persuade my husband to do anything against his will.

"I am sorry, Richard," Anthony replied with a note of regret. "I can no longer live under the same roof as a traitor such as her."

I watched Richard's expression turn to contempt as he stood watching his cousin before he replied.

"Very well," he said at last. "You had best leave in the morning, earlier if possible."

Anthony looked taken aback, as though he had not expected him to put me first. Did he not understand even now what we meant to each other?

"You are really taking her side?" He protested. "You have raised me, been like a father to me, and you would take the side of a treacherous heretic over me?"

I saw Richard's fist clench dangerously and wondered just where this was going to lead.

"My wife," he said, "is a Protestant, not a heretic. And I have not only forgiven her, we have forgiven each other."

"And what of Rachel?" Anthony demanded with a sly glance of satisfaction at me. "Will you simply abandon her now? Is this a day when I must learn you will abandon anyone who gets in your way?"

He expected some sort of reaction from me, that was obvious. He had no idea what Richard had told me, he did not know the role Rachel played in his life and believed he would be hurting me by mentioning her.

"You have no idea about Rachel," Richard shouted. "You had best not speak her name before me, after everything she has done for us."

That is when I made up my mind. I knew he would not abandon her, that he would do what she wished and I badly needed to know what that was.

I stepped between them and turned to face my husband.

"I want to meet her," I said.

***

I was very nervous as the carriage took us the short distance to Rachel's house. During that journey, Richard held my hand and told me this beautiful woman of whom I had been so jealous for so long, was his dearest friend and he hoped she would be mine as well.

"I am not sure I can do that, Richard," I said. "I will try, but you need to understand how much I have loathed her. All this time, as far as I knew, she had stolen away the man I loved. Do you know how I came to be in London when Julia was executed?"

"No. It never even occurred to me to wonder."

"I went to London to spy on you. When Anthony told me you had presented another woman to the Queen as Lady Summerville, I was so angry, so devastated, I had to see for myself how you were with her. I followed you from the palace gates, I saw you laughing together and I was convinced she was the love of your life, that I was nothing but a breeding vessel."

He pulled me close and kissed me.

"I am so sorry."

"Had I the opportunity, I would cheerfully have killed her. It will not be easy to change those feelings, not even for you."

"You will try, though?"

"Of course. She saved my life. I would not be here were it not for her; just do not expect too much, please."

As we waited for the little maid to announce us, my heart began to beat faster and when I saw Rachel up close, all my doubts came brimming to the surface. Could it really be possible that these two had not been lovers, despite what he told me? How could he have resisted her?

She stood up and her eyes held Richard's before she said in an accusing tone:

"You told her."

CHAPTER FOURTEEN

Rachel's Journal

When Louisa led them into my little sitting room, she was blushing and looking at the floor. I doubt she ever thought she would be announcing Lady Summerville in this house.

"Lord and Lady Summerville," she announced, then fled to the kitchen.

I got slowly to my feet and my eyes held Richard's.

"You told her," I said at once.

"Rachel, I had to," he said pleadingly. "I wanted us to have an honest new start. I know I have let you down, that they were your secrets to tell. Will you forgive me?"

I felt very uncomfortable having this conversation in front of Bethany. What must she must think of me? I was afraid to talk to him with my usual familiarity lest it offend her. Richard had parted with my secrets to make her believe there had been nothing between him and me, but had it worked? Did she believe it, or did I have in my house a woman who believed I was her husband's mistress?

She studied me carefully, her dark eyes sweeping over my face as though trying to see into my soul, into my heart, trying to decide whether to believe what she had been told. How hard was it going to be for her to accept that her handsome, virile husband had treated me as a sister all these years? Even when he was sharing his apartments in the palace with me? I knew I did not look the innocent, I never had; I only wished I could.

After a glance at Richard, as though seeking approval, she stepped forward and took both my hands in hers.

"Is it true?" She asked softly.

"Yes, it is," I answered carefully, wondering whether I would now be called a liar.

Then she let go of my hands and put her arms around me, hugging me close.

"I feel for you, My Lady," she said gently. "Richard tells me you have done me a great service, quite possibly saved my life. I thank you from the bottom of my heart, for both of us."

While we stood so close together, I could feel her trembling and her pulse racing, I could almost feel the doubt that remained.

"I was happy to do it," I said. "I do not suppose in his modesty, Richard told you what he has done for me over the years."

I picked up the rolled up parchment that Richard had sent to me and gave it to her.

"Perhaps this will convince you, My Lady," I said.

She stood and read the letter, her expression changing from one of doubt to one of sorrow. I looked past her at her husband and saw him mouth the words "thank you" for the second time that day.

I gestured them both to sit down and poured wine. I was running out of things to say and I was afraid of saying the wrong thing. Apparently, he had persuaded her that our relationship was always purely platonic, but we still loved each other and I was afraid she might see that and take it to mean he had lied.

"I will return to Finsbury, My Lady," I said as soon as we were seated. "I do not want the villagers to start their gossip again."

"I do not care what they think," she said. "Of course, if you will be happier there, then that is one thing, but please do not leave on my account. I owe you a debt that can never be repaid, not only in taking my place at court, but in persuading my husband that I did not go out of my way to betray him."

My eyes met hers and I felt humbled by the love she so obviously had for him. Did I really convince him? Was it only my word, or did he understand why she did what she did?

I wished I could have stayed, wished we could have been friends. But I knew the people here would never believe the truth. They would not welcome me and they would soon pity her.

"People here believe they know what I have been, and nothing anyone says is going to change that. If I stay, they will resent me and they will resent Richard. I will be better in Finsbury, where nobody knows me as Richard's mistress." I watched her expression and thought I saw a frown of suspicion cross her lovely features. I could almost hear her wondering if this was some plot to keep me in her husband's bed, wondering if she was being made a fool of. If the letter did not convince her, nothing would. "If I stay, I will come between you. I will not allow that."

She turned to Richard and said something which surprised me.

"Could you leave us, please? Do you mind?"

He too looked surprised but he left the room and I heard the front door open and close behind him. Now I was the one trembling, wondering what it was she wanted to say that she could not say in front of him.

"Are you not convinced?" I asked her. "Even seeing his last request to me?"

"I believe you," she replied quietly. "It is not easy, but I do believe you. And I think I understand why you did not want anyone to know the truth, why you did not want people whispering about you."

"What then? What troubles you, My Lady?"

"He says he loves me," she replied simply. "Does he speak the truth? Has he really forgiven me?"

It was my turn to take her hands.

"Oh, My Lady!" I said. "He loves you more than anything in the world. He was prepared to die for you. You must never doubt him, never."

"Thank you," she said softly, squeezing my hands. "I hope we will meet again. I hope you will call on us before you return to Finsbury. I know that Richard will want to see you again."

Then she was gone, leaving me to envy her the future she would have with the only man I could ever have loved.

THE END

Author's Note: Thank you for reading Holy Poison: The Judas Pledge. I hope you have enjoyed it and if you have, please leave a review on the Amazon website.

Don't miss the other five books in the series.

please consider my other books:

The Romany Princess
The Gorston Widow
The Crusader's Widow
The Wronged Wife
To Catch a Demon
The Adulteress
Conquest
The Loves of the Lionheart
The Cavalier's Pact
The Minstrel's Lady (winner of 2017 e festival of words Best Romance)
A Man in Mourning

Pestilence Series:

The Second Wife
The Scent of Roses
Once Loved (winner 2017 e festival of words Best Historical)

The Elizabethans:

The Earl's Jealousy
The Viscount's Divorce
Lord John's Folly

The Hartleighs of Somersham

A Match of Honour
Lady Penelope's Frenchman

Non-historical

Old Fashioned Values
Mirielle

If you would like to receive notification of future publications, as well as some free books, click here.